CHICAGO

HOMICIDE

BY

John C. Dalglish

2016

CHICAGO HOMICIDE

<u>Monday, September 1</u>
<u>Labor Day</u>

A Chicago Park
11:45 p.m.

He stopped the car, killed the lights, and scanned the area around him. The leaves hadn't started their seasonal descent to the ground, and a light breeze rustled them just enough to cover any noise he might make. Reassured there was no one around, he popped the trunk. Going around to the back, he scanned the parking area once more, then lifted the trunk lid.

Moving quickly now, he hooked his hands under the armpits of his lifeless victim and dragged her out of the car. Her feet dropped to the pavement with a dull thud. Dragging her across the lot, only the scraping of her tennis shoes on the gravel broke the silence. He'd scouted and memorized his route, and in less than a minute, he emerged onto a riverbank.

His shoes quickly soaked through as he backed into the rivers current enough to let her head drop in the water. Moving around to her legs, he removed her shoes and pitched them into the river. Next, he grabbed the waistband of her pants and pulled them down to her ankles.

Now for my signatures.

Grabbing the knife on his belt, he cut her panties loose, pulled them from the body, and stuffed them into his jeans pocket. Finally, he reached down and tore something off the front of her t-shirt. He examined the tiny item briefly before prying open the girl's mouth, and forcing it in.

Standing back, he surveyed the scene. With her hair splayed out around her partially submerged head, and her pale skin reflecting the moonlight, it was just as he'd imagined. He worked to fix the image in his mind.

It's perfect.

He started back up the path toward his car.

Now, to make the phone call.

<u>Tuesday, September 2</u>

Apartment of Chad Marshall
Balmoral Avenue
6:05 a.m.

Chad Marshall climbed out of bed and, feeling more than seeing his way into the kitchen, got his morning coffee started. Back in the bedroom, he made his way to the bathroom and splashed water on his face. Twenty minutes later, he'd showered, shaved, and returned to the coffee pot. Opening the fridge, he discovered a note under the creamer. It was from Christie, his live-in girlfriend. *Love you—see you tonight. C.S.*

He tucked the note in his pocket as he poured his creamer, then took his cup and phone to a worn brown recliner in the living room. Scrolling through his email, reading a few but deleting most, he moved on to his voicemail.

"First message — '*Morning, Chad. Don't forget we have the early production meeting.*' —End of message one."

His producer, Vince Henderson, made a practice of reminding him at least three times for each appointment on their schedule. He was well acquainted with his reporter's habit of becoming distracted and forgetting important meetings. He deleted the message and moved on to the next.

"Second message — *'Take the Zoo Woods south entrance, drive to the first curve, get out and walk toward the river. You will find her body there.'* — End of second message."

Chad stared at his phone. The voice was impossible to recognize, but the tone of the call compelled him to take it seriously. This was no joke, and just might be a huge story.

Addison Avenue "L" Station
Brown Line
North Center
7:10 a.m.

Vince Henderson checked his watch as he made his way off the train and down to the street. The walk from the train station to WWND, just over ten blocks, was nice this time of year. September in Chicago brought relief from the oppressive heat of summer, but was still far enough from the approaching winter. It allowed him to treasure the days without the overwhelming dread of the coming cold.

A warm breeze had replaced the early morning chill, and he stopped to remove his hoodie before picking up the pace. He wanted to be on time for the eight o'clock production meeting. A newly minted associate producer with WWND-10, the Chicago ABC affiliate, he looked forward to each new day and each new assignment. As the youngest associate producer, he rarely got the exciting events to cover. Nevertheless, he was getting his feet wet and learning on the fly.

WWND's home was a large warehouse-like structure, beige and boring on the outside, but vibrant and fast-paced within. It was like stepping off an escalator and onto a bullet train.

Vince swiped his station ID badge and entered the hallway leading back to his office. Reds and tans swirled together on a carpet leading down white hallways to a series of offices. His was the first on the right, where he deposited his briefcase and grabbed his coffee mug.

Stopping long enough to glance in the mirror on the back of his door, he checked his appearance before the meeting. At just twenty-nine, and with no thanks to his father's genetics, his hair was already thinning. Two years ago, he'd shaved his head completely. He liked the look, and figured if it was good enough for Michael Jordan, it was good enough for him. Light brown skin and dark green eyes, combined with his trim shape, brought him plenty of attention from the ladies.

As he filled his cup at the coffee maker, he spotted his reporter finally arriving. Chad approached with his usual vibrating energy. "Morning, Vince."

"Morning, Chad."

"So Vince, I've got something I want you to hear."

"Another one of your jokes?"

The reporter ignored the jab. "No, no. I got a creepy voicemail on my phone and I think you should listen to it."

Chad, like his A.P., was green. He made up for his inexperience with his constant forward motion in the perpetual chase of a "big" story. That energy had snared him a breaking kidnap situation at his previous job that caught the eye of the brass at WWND.

Vince checked his watch, then studied his partner. "Meeting is about to start. Can't it wait?"

"No, I don't think so. It could be a huge story."

"Are you two planning on joining us?"

The two men swiveled to see News Director Reilly glaring at them. Vince shrugged at Chad. "I guess it will *have* to wait."

The pair made a beeline for the door and took their seats.

Forty minutes later, they were back in Vince's office, where they found the third member of their team waiting for them.

Tommy Castillo served as the camera and sound tech on all their shoots. At just twenty-three, his standard work uniform consisted of a muscle shirt and cargo shorts. Born in Brazil, his skin was perpetually exposed to the elements of Chicago's weather, including the cold. To his partner's amazement, the young cameraman wore the same thing most of the winter as well.

Tommy grinned up at them from a chair by the window. "Morning, fellas. What have we got to sink our teeth into today?"

"Closing of the city pools."

Tommy rolled his eyes. "You're kidding, right?"

"Nope."

"That sucks."

Chad was busy playing with his phone. "I've got something you guys should hear."

9

Vince sat behind his desk. "What is it?"

"It's the message I told you about."

"Oh, goodie."

Ignoring the sarcasm dripping from his producer's voice, Chad hit the button.

"Take the Zoo Woods south entrance, drive to the first curve, get out and walk toward the river. You will find her body there."

Chad stopped the playback. "Like I said... creepy, huh?"

Vince grinned at Tommy. "Sounds like a practical joke to me."

Tommy laughed. "Me too."

Chad would not be swayed. "I don't think so. Listen again."

He replayed the message.

"Did you notice the voice was disguised electronically? Why do that for a prank when a sock over the receiver will do?"

Vince was still not buying it. "If it's not a joke, then it's probably just some nut job who got your number."

"Maybe, but I don't think so. Let's take the truck and check it out."

Vince held up his hands in defeat. "Look, let's get our pool shoot done, then we'll see."

Momentarily appeased, Chad put away his phone. "Fair enough."

Humboldt Park Pool
Sacramento Ave
8:30 a.m.

The day was warm and the sun reflected off Chad's face as he stared into the camera. After handing a microphone to the reporter, Tommy moved behind the camera to confirm he had the best shot.

Chad smiled broadly, his tortoise-shell glasses and sandy-brown hair giving him an intellectual appearance that was in contrast to his warm, friendly voice. He was nothing if not smooth on camera, and most of the time they got the story done in just one take.

Tommy had framed Chad with the pool in the background, and after Vince double-checked the shot, he pointed at his on-camera talent. "Go."

"I'm standing in front of the Humboldt Park Pool, one of fifty outdoor pools scattered across the city. The pool sits empty this morning, the slide absent of kids, the

11

deck void of sunbathers. The reason? With the passing of the Labor Day holiday, this and the other forty-nine outdoor pools in the Chicago Parks system have officially closed for the season. A sure sign that fall has arrived."

Tommy had shot some school bus video earlier in the morning and Vince would edit the footage in at this point.

"School busses make their way around the city now, gathering their charges for another busy academic year, and the campuses of Chicago's more than twenty universities now teem with activity. There is no mistaking the acceleration of September as we leave the slower pace of summer behind.

With the full school busses, and the beginning of the Bears and Blackhawks seasons, we acknowledge the end of another hot summer in Chicago. Reporting for WWND-10, from Humboldt Park, this is Chad Marshall."

Chad held the microphone in place for an extra few seconds, then dropped it along with his smile. "Look good, Tommy?"

"It did to me. How'd it sound, Vince?"

"Pretty good. Let me watch it back in the truck before we pack up."

Chad pulled out his phone as Vince climbed into the white production van. He and Tommy listened to the voicemail twice more. Tommy was beginning to come around to the reporter's side. "I have to admit, it kind of gives me a chill."

"I know, right?"

Vince stuck his head out of the van. "It's good. Pack it up."

"Awesome. You guys ready to go to Zoo Woods with me?"

Vince shook his head. "Not me. I've got editing to do."

"Tommy, you want to go?"

"I'd love to, but I have a lunch date with a young thing that looks a lot better than you do!"

Chad shrugged. "Okay. I guess I'll fly solo on this one."

Chicago Police Department Area 5 Precinct 8:30 a.m.

Detective Reginald Brown turned his black Chevy Impala into the parking lot at Area 5 Precinct. Early as usual, Reggie parked in the same spot he'd used for the last twelve years, ever since transferring in as a Homicide detective. Checking the mirror, his curly hair was now more gray than black. His dark skin and brown eyes showed the wear of his thirty years with Chicago PD.

Not much longer now.

He sighed and pushed open his car door. Folding his six-foot-four, two-hundred-twenty-pound frame out of the car, he stretched upward before heading to the precinct's side door.

The non-descript, single-story building looked more like a library than a police station, with tan brick below cement-framed windows. He swiped his badge at the officer's entrance and made his way through the halls to his cubicle. Before he could sit down, his day started.

"Reggie!"

Stopping in his tracks, he turned to look through the open door of his lieutenant's office. Just a few years younger than Reggie, the lieutenant bore a graying moustache to match his graying curly hair. "Good morning, sir."

Lieutenant Jerry Davis grinned at his long-time friend. "No reason to sit down; I've got a scene I need you at."

"Yes, sir." Reggie moved into the office and accepted the piece of paper held out to him. "What have we got?"

"Single female, Zoo Woods Park. I need you out there twenty minutes ago."

Reggie raised an eyebrow. "Okay. What's the rush?"

"This one was called in by Chad Marshall."

"Chad Marshall of WWND—that Chad Marshall?"

"That's the one, and for all I know, pictures of the body are already on the air!"

"I'll leave immediately. Is there a patrol on the scene?"

"Yes, and the coroner is on route as well."

"Okay boss. I'm on it."

Film Editing Room
WWND-10 Studios
North Center
8:40 a.m.

Vince had just loaded some tape in the editing machine when his cell phone rang.

"Hello?"

"Vince! It's Chad."

"Hey. Did you get my email on the pool thing?"

"Never mind that. Is Tommy there?"

"Somewhere. Why?"

Chad's voice was several octaves higher than normal. "Grab Tommy, jump in the video truck, and get over here!"

"Where?"

"Zoo Woods!"

"Why?"

"Why! Because the message was real, that's why!"

"You found a… Come on, you're pulling my leg, right?"

"Dog gone it, Vince, I'm not kidding. I'm at the scene of a murder and you need to get here now."

"I'm on my way."

16

Zoo Woods Park
South 1ˢᵗ Avenue
9:05 a.m.

Tommy Castillo pulled the white van, with WWND-10 emblazoned across the side panels in big blue letters, to a stop behind Chad's car.

Vince climbed out to find Chad running toward him. Yellow crime tape flapped in the breeze at the edge of the parking lot as a uniformed officer stood guard. Chad was flushed with anxiety. "You're here! I was sure channel four or nine would beat you."

"What have we got?"

Chad pushed his iPhone in front of his producer's face. "This."

Vince stared at the photo, then jerked backward. "Shoot, Chad! Warn a guy, will ya?"

"Oh, sorry."

Vince took the phone from his reporter and examined the photo closer. A dark-haired girl lay at the side of the river, her hair wet, and her eyes lifeless. Jogging pants had been pulled down around her ankles and her t-shirt was pulled partway up. "Could you tell how she died?"

"Strangulation. There was a clear set of marks on her neck."

"Do the police know you have this shot?"

"No. I got it before the patrol officers arrived."

Vince handed the phone to Tommy, who had just joined them. Tommy examined it quickly, then handed it to Chad. "Gruesome."

A black Impala pulled up behind the TV truck. Chad tucked his phone in his jacket pocket. "Looks like they sent Brown."

Vince looked at the detective getting out of the Impala, then back at his reporter. "You know we can't use that photo on the air, right?"

"I know that. Still, it gives us information the other stations don't have."

Vince looked around him; they were standing on a tree-lined drive that looped through a few acres of woods. "How did you find her?"

"I followed the directions on the voicemail. Once I cleared the brush and came out on the bank, she was right there."

"You have to tell the detective about that."

"What do you have to tell the detective?" Reggie Brown had joined their circle.

Vince nodded. "Hey, detective. I'll let Chad fill you in."

Reggie turned toward the reporter and waited. Chad nodded at the detective. "I was the one who called in the body."

"So I heard. How did you come to find her?"

"A voicemail."

"The dead woman left you a voicemail?"

Chad grinned, but Reggie wasn't smiling. "No, no. Of course not. I don't know who left the voicemail, but it told me I would find a body here."

"I see. Can I hear it?"

"Sure." Chad took his phone out and replayed the message.

Reggie had him play it back three more times. "I'll need you to stop by the station with that later."

"Of course."

The detective stared hard at the reporter. "Have you got anything else I need to know about?"

Chad shook his head, avoiding his producer's glare. "Nope. We were just getting ready to do a report."

19

Reggie studied him a moment longer, then turned to go. "Don't let me see anything on the air I shouldn't, gentlemen."

When he had walked away, Tommy let out a low whistle. "You're walking a fine line, buddy."

Vince was a little more emphatic in his description. "More like a high-wire over the Grand Canyon without a net." He moved toward the back of the truck. "Alright, let's get set up. We'll use the yellow tape in the background and do a live hook-up with the station.
"

Bank of Des Moines River
Zoo Woods
9:20 a.m.

The coroner's van had showed up while Reggie was listening to the tape, and he found several crime scene techs already around the body when he got to the riverbank. A photographer snapped away while Coroner Janet Thorsen waited her opportunity to examine the body. "Hey, Reggie."

"Hi, Janet."

Janet Thorsen had been coroner of Cook County for seven years, and Reggie was always glad when she showed up rather than of one of her assistants. Her meticulous work could help him make sense of the most complicated scene.

Short, brown hair and pale skin from spending more time in the morgue than in fresh air, she was brilliant in all aspects of her field. Her lively green eyes, like her personality, were sharp and focused. Coroner Thorsen was all business, all the time.

Before he retired, Reggie was determined to make her smile just once while working a crime scene. He was running out of time. "Lovely day on the river, huh?"

"Not for her." No smile.

Reggie pulled out his notepad and studied the scene. The girl was in her late teens or early twenties, with brown hair that sloshed in the river's current. Her black t-shirt was rolled up, exposing her stomach, and her jogging pants were around her ankles. White socks but no shoes.

Reggie looked around him, then noticed a police officer making notes of his own. "Were you first on the scene?"

"Yes, sir. Officer Hadley."

"Did you find any identification?"

"No sir."

"Has a search of the area been conducted?"

"It's ongoing, but nothing has turned up yet."

"Okay. Tell the searchers the victim's shoes and underwear are missing."

"I'll pass it on."

The photographer having finished, Janet stepped in. After a brief examination, she looked back at the detective. "Death appears to be strangulation; possibly some sort of garrote. Death was at least twelve hours ago, probably not more than twenty-four. I'll have to confirm those observations at autopsy, along with checking to see if there was a sexual assault."

"What's your hunch?"

"If I had to guess—no."

Reggie looked up and down the riverbank. "Any chance she floated here?"

"Judging from her skin, probably not. It doesn't show signs of being in the water for any length of time."

"Makes sense, and fits with the scene. There seems to be a trail down from the parking lot, although I can't say for sure if it was from the killer, or our own people."

The coroner rolled the girl on her side, checking for wounds to the back of her torso. "Here's something."

Reggie leaned closer. "What?"

"She's got a tattoo on her lower back."

"A tramp stamp?"

Janet flashed him a quick look. "A dolphin."

Reggie ignored the coroner's disapproval and made a note. "See any others?"

Janet pulled the victim's socks down on both feet. "Yes, left ankle. A heart."

Reggie spotted the photographer not far away. "Hey! Can I get a couple extra shots over here?"

The young female officer came back over. "What have you got?"

Reggie pointed at the coroner. "Miss Thorsen looks particularly nice today; let's get a shot of our coroner hard at work."

Janet rolled her eyes, and Reggie thought she was just about to smile, but it didn't happen. Janet pointed at the heart tattoo and the photographer snapped a couple, then she rolled the body to expose the dolphin for a couple more shots.

When the officer was done, Reggie smiled at her. "What's your name?"

"Rodriguez, Naomi Rodriguez."

"Sorry about yelling at you. I'm Detective Brown."

The photographer smiled at the gesture. As she walked away, Reggie turned back to Janet. "Any sign of blunt force trauma?"

She shook her head. "I can give you a more definitive answer after the autopsy, but I've got three bodies ahead of her at the morgue. I should get to her by tomorrow morning."

"Okay. Thanks, Doc."

Reggie followed the trail back up to the parking lot just in time to see Chad Marshall starting a live report.

The reporter, his sandy-brown hair covered by a blue WWND-10 ball cap, stood in front of the yellow crime tape. With a matching blue WWND jacket over a polo shirt, khaki pants, and tortoise-shell glasses, he struck Reggie as more college dean than reporter.

Seizing the opportunity, Reggie circled the TV truck and got back to his car without any more questions from the now growing number of press vehicles and personnel.

*Office of
Lieutenant Jerry Davis
Area 5 Precinct
1:15 p.m.*

After grabbing a Starbucks grande coffee, Reggie had returned to the station. Lieutenant Davis waved at him to come into his office, again before Reggie could sit down.

"What have we got, Reggie?"

"Female, late teens or early twenties, strangled."

"How did Marshall come to find the body?"

"Voicemail."

"From the dead girl?"

Reggie laughed at hearing his own joke replayed. "No. An unidentified caller left directions to the body on Marshall's voicemail."

"You're kidding?"

"Nope. I listened to it few times and he's bringing me a copy later."

"What about an ID?"

"Nothing on the victim, and we haven't turned anything up in the area searches so far. I have a basic description along with two tattoos located on her body."

Jerry Davis smiled at him. "So, now the fun starts."

Reggie rolled his eyes and started for the door. "Just remember, I'm on a countdown clock."

"Counting down the days, huh?"

"Not me, Sonya. And she's counting by the hours!"

Jerry laughed. "Your wife has been waiting thirty years for this. She's not gonna give up an extra minute!"

"That's right. When midnight strikes on September fifteenth, this detective turns into a retired pumpkin."

****

Two hours later, Reggie still hadn't found a single missing persons report with a description matching his victim.

"Detective Brown?"

Reggie looked up to see Chad Marshall standing at his desk. "Hey, Chad. Thanks for coming in."

"Sure. Sorry it took so long. I had to do a live report for the noon news."

"No problem. Let's make a duplicate of that message, okay?"

Chad got out his phone and handed it to him. "It's the first one on the list. Just press play."

Reggie stood. "Good. I'll be right back."

Taking the reporter's phone and going into an interview room, he played the message onto a small voice recorder. Satisfied his copy was of high enough quality, he returned to his desk where he laid the phone in front of Chad. "You have time for a couple questions?"

Chad retrieved his phone and checked to make sure it was still on the voicemail screen. "Sure."

"When was the first time you listened to it?"

"Around six-thirty, I think."

"This morning or last night?"

"This morning. The message wasn't there until after I went to bed last night."

Reggie nodded and scribbled a couple notes. "Have you received any others like it before this?"

"Not from this person."

"What do you mean?"

Chad smirked. "I get emails and messages from crackpots fairly often; most reporters do."

27

Reggie raised an eyebrow. "On your personal phone?"

"Uh… well, not usually."

"How about the voice? Do you recognize it?"

Chad shook his head. "Not with that distortion they're using. I'm not sure if it's a man or a woman. Are you?"

Reggie had to agree. "It's pretty tough to tell. I need you to do one more thing for me."

"What's that?"

"Contact your phone carrier and get the number that left the message."

Chad checked his watch. "It'll have to be later. I've got a meeting at two-thirty."

"That's fine." Reggie took out one of his business cards and slid it across the desk. "Call me when you get it."

Chad stood. "No problem."

"I watched your report at Zoo Woods. You referred to the message as 'information' and not as a voicemail. Can we keep that fact under wraps for now?"

"I suppose. I'll just refer to it as a source, if you like."

"I appreciate it."

"Sure." Chad headed out.

Watching him leave, Reggie realized he'd forgotten something. "Chad!"

The reporter turned. "Yeah?"

Reggie caught up with him. "Let me see the card I gave you."

Chad handed it over. Reggie scrawled on the back and returned it to him. "That's my personal number. If you get any further communication from the messenger, call me immediately."

"I will."

****

Reggie shut off the TV in the lieutenant's office. After spending the entire afternoon going through missing persons and coming up empty, he'd stayed to watch Chad's six o'clock news report. While the reporter had danced all around it, he'd kept his promise and not revealed the source came through a voicemail.

The phone on his desk rang and he scrambled to get it. "Homicide—Brown."

"Yes, Detective. This is Chad Marshall."

"Hey, Chad. I watched your report. Nice job."

"Thanks. I have that phone number for you."

Reggie grabbed a piece of paper. "Excellent. Shoot."

Chad read it off to him.

When he was finished, Reggie thanked him and hung up. He immediately dialed the number.

"I'm sorry, but the number you have reached is no longer in service. Please re-check the number and..."

Reggie hung up. He had expected as much, which meant he now needed a warrant to get more information from the phone carrier. He filled out the paperwork and left it on the lieutenant's desk.

Rubbing his neck and acknowledging his exhaustion, it was clear he'd reached a point where nothing more of value could be done tonight. He clicked off his desk light and headed for the black Impala.

<u>Wednesday, September 3</u>

*Home of
Sonya & Reggie Brown
Eastside Neighborhood
7:00 a.m.*

Sonya Brown moved her five-foot frame around the small kitchen with vigor and efficiency. Born in Puerto Rico, she had moved to Georgia with her parents when she was a child. Fate and a scholarship had brought her to Chicago, where the rest as they say, was history.

"Reggie, breakfast is ready!"

A plate of eggs and toast was waiting for him at the table, along with his wife of thirty-eight years. He kissed her forehead and sat down to eat. Sipping her coffee, she watched him over the top of her mug. "Twelve days left."

He smiled, now accustomed to the countdown. "How many hours is that?"

She smiled at his teasing. "Too many!"

They sat in a comfortable silence while he finished. Many fellow officers had marriages begin and end during his years with Chicago PD, but he'd been one of the lucky few. Sonya was his best friend in the truest sense. Knocking him down when he needed it and picking him up when he needed that.

He checked his watch. "I've got to get going."

"What's your day look like?"

"It starts with an autopsy at eight sharp."

She laughed. "Well, it can only go uphill from there!"

"You're right about that! I'll call later when I know what time I'll be home."

She stood and cleared his plate. He watched her with the same combination of affection and awe he'd experienced the first time he'd met her.

She'd been studying for her teaching degree at Loyola University at the same time he was pursuing Criminal Justice at Robert Morris. A mutual friend introduced them and he was immediately smitten. From that moment on, her wavy black hair and big brown eyes had convinced him no one else would do.

One daughter, a paid-off mortgage, two careers nearing completion, and hundreds of treasured moments later, they were preparing for the most anticipated time of their life together.

He pulled himself up out of the chair, accepted his travel mug of coffee and a kiss, then headed out the door.

*Office of
the Medical Examiner
Cook County
Harrison Street
7:55 a.m.*

Located in the Near West Side, roughly ten minutes from the Chicago loop and only blocks from the United Center, the Medical Examiner's Office took up a big chunk of downtown Chicago. Surrounded by black wrought-iron fence, the modern concrete structure was an imposing member of the Chicago Technology Park.

Reggie found his way to the observation room just as Janet Thorsen, dressed in blue scrubs, came into the autopsy suite. She spotted him, gave a little wave, and punched the com-box button. "Here for the early show?"

He keyed the mic. "I believe in starting the day off right."

She nodded and moved over to the table where their victim lay stretched out. Flipping the overhead microphone on, she began the practiced ritual of dissecting and recording.

"Case number ME-155, female victim, body found at Zoo Woods. Janet Thorsen conducting."

Reggie could listen in as she worked, but he wouldn't be able to ask questions until she was done. He pulled up a stool and settled in. He'd lost count of how many autopsies he'd seen in his career, but the process was still amazing to him.

When he'd started at CPD, most of the science they used to solve cases now hadn't yet been dreamed up. DNA was the biggest development, but what the coroner could learn from a body these days was staggering.

Janet moved methodically, taking another set of photos, doing a complete external examination, trimming fingernails and bagging them, then turning the body over and repeating the process. Returning the body to a face-up position, she moved in especially close to the strangulation marks, spending several minutes on them.

Apparently satisfied with her exam, she moved her attention to the girl's face, and pried the jaw open. Pausing briefly, she then turned and grabbed a set of tweezers from the stainless tray beside her. Reaching down into the back of the throat, she extracted a small pink object.

Holding it up to the light, then turning to show it to him, Reggie jumped up to get a closer look. After staring hard, he held up his hands and mouthed: *Can't see.*

Janet moved over to the observation glass and held it up for the detective to get a closer look. He recognized it immediately, having seen something similar on his daughter.

A sorority pledge pin!

He gave Janet a thumbs up, then sat back down. His victim was almost certainly a college girl, but was the pin hers or the killer's? And how did it get in her mouth?

He would have to wait until the coroner was done to get a better look at the pin, but his mind was already cycling through the over two dozen universities in the Chicago area, and the student population in excess of six hundred thousand.

His search had just narrowed and expanded at the same time.

****

Forty-five minutes later, Reggie and Janet were sitting in her office. He held the baggie containing the pin up to the light. "It's going to take ages to identify the sorority."

Janet laughed. "That's what Google is for."

"You're right about that. What else did we learn?"

She looked down at her notes. "Death by strangulation was confirmed. My hunch is a double-loop garrote was used."

Reggie's eyebrows lifted. "A double-loop?"

"Yeah. Instead of a single wire attached to two handles, the wire is looped, making a continuous circle through the handles."

Reggie couldn't remember a case where he'd seen one. "Why the double-loop?"

"If the victim gets a finger or thumb between one of the loops and their throat, pulling on it only tightens the other loop. The victim essentially helps the killer strangle them."

Reggie shook his head. "That's nasty. What else?"

"I was able to get semen samples, but there weren't signs of forced penetration. My guess is she had consensual sex with someone in the hours before she died. I'll run a DNA screen anyway, along with one for the fingernail scrapings."

Reggie was making his own notes. "T.O.D. still consistent with your first impression?"

"Yes, and there was no water in the lungs, so she was dead before her head was dropped in the river."

Reggie stood. "Okay, thanks Doc."

"Sure. I'll forward the report to your desk."

"Great. Oh, by the way, any other tattoos?"

Janet shook her head. "Just the two we found on scene."

"Good enough." He turned to leave.

"Hey, when's your last day, Reggie?"

"September fifteenth."

"Well, solve this before then, will ya? I don't want to be educating a rookie in the middle of a case."

He laughed. "I'll do what I can!"

"That's all any of us can do, right?"

"Truer words were never spoken."

Homicide Squad Room
Area 5 Precinct
10:15 a.m.

Back at his desk, his travel mug refilled with fresh coffee, Reggie fired up his computer. He entered the phrase *US Sororities* into the search field. A list of nearly one hundred registered sororities from across the country popped up instantly. The pin taken from the victim's mouth consisted of a pink triangle with the letters Γ Σ Δ in red across it. Going down the list, he was able to find the symbols, and the corresponding sorority — Gamma Sigma Delta.

That was easier than I thought!

A new search of the sorority name produced a link to their webpage and a list of member chapters. Four area universities showed up. Loyola, DePaul, Robert Morris, and the Central College of Chicago. Reaching into his desk drawer, Reggie found the list of phone numbers he kept for the security offices at each school. Starting with Loyola, he dialed.

"Loyola Security. Norton."

"Yes, this is Detective Reggie Brown from Chicago PD."

"Hey, Detective. How can we help you?"

"Do you guys have any reports of a missing female?"

"Not that I'm aware of. Hold on."

Less than a minute later, Norton returned to the phone. "Nothing active right now, Detective. Why do you ask?"

"We've got an unidentified girl in our morgue and I believe she's an area college student."

"Well, she's not ours. At least, not as far as we know."

"Okay, thanks."

After hanging up, Reggie drew a line through Loyola on his list. Dialing DePaul next, he repeated the process, unfortunately with the same results. DePaul got crossed off and he was about to dial Robert Morris when a sheet of paper landed on his desk.

"There are the results from your phone subpoena."

Reggie looked up at his lieutenant, then back at the single sheet of paper. "That's it?"

"Afraid so. The call to Marshall's phone was the only one made from that number, which was tied to a prepaid throwaway phone. No information was provided when it was purchased and activated."

"What about the tower it pinged during the call?"

"It's there."

Reggie scanned to the bottom of the printout and found the tower designation. "Grant Park."

Davis nodded. "That's right. So, was it a tourist, a businessman, or a resident enjoying the view of Lake Michigan? It's anybody's guess."

The detective grunted and rubbed his neck. It wasn't even lunch yet and he could feel a headache coming on. When he removed his hand, blood was on his fingers. "What the…?"

The lieutenant stared at him. "You cut yourself?"

Reggie grabbed a Kleenex and wiped the spot. "No. I've got a spot on my neck that irritates me, but it's never bled before."

"You should have it looked at."

"I suppose. I've identified the sorority pin found in our victim's mouth. Four universities in the area have a chapter, and I've already spoken with two of them. So far, no luck."

"Okay. Let me know if you need anything."

"Thanks, boss."

The phone on Reggie's desk rang. "Homicide. Detective Brown."

"Good morning, Detective. My name is Frank Washington."

"What can I do for you, Mr. Washington?"

"I'm a security officer with CCC…"

"I'm sorry, did you say CCC?"

"Yes, sir. Central College of Chicago."

Reggie's gaze flicked to the list of schools in front of him. "Yes, of course. How can I help you?"

"I have a missing girl report here at the school, and as a matter of course, we check police stations, hospitals, morgues, and the like. A Doctor Thorsen at the morgue told me I should call you."

Reggie's pulse quickened. "Do you have a name?"

"Mackenzie Addison."

Reggie wrote the name down. "Her description?"

"White, nineteen, brown hair."

"Any tattoos?"

"Two. A dolphin and a heart."

Reggie just got his first break. "I hate to say this, but that matches the description of a Jane Doe in our morgue. When did she go missing?"

There was a hesitation on the other end of the phone. "Crap… Labor Day."

The baggie with the pin caught his eye. "Washington… is that what you said your name was?"

"Yeah, but Frank is fine."

"Frank, was Miss Addison pledging a sorority?"

The officer's surprise was evident. "As a matter of fact, yes. A sorority sister reported her missing."

"What sorority was it?"

"Gamma Sigma Delta. Why?"

"Our Jane Doe had a sorority pin in her possession. Do you think the girl who reported her missing could identify the body?"

"I imagine, but I'm not sure."

"Okay, Frank. I'm on my way over with some photos. Can you see if she's available?"

"Of course."

"And Frank…"

"Yeah?"

"Let's keep the status of Miss Addison quiet for now. Just tell the friend you need her help."

"Will do."

Reggie hung up and went in to talk to Lieutenant Davis. Twenty minutes later, he was on I-90, heading northwest toward the college.

Security Offices
Central College of Chicago
Norwood Park
11:45 a.m.

The sprawling, fifty-two-acre campus of CCC was idyllic. Wide green lawns shaded by the fall colors of gold and yellow from American elm trees. The structures reminded Reggie of old English mansions, brownstone brick with white stone trimming the windows and doors. He would not have been surprised to find a moat around the campus.

After parking near the administration building, he asked a passerby for directions to Frank Washington's office. Once inside the security headquarters, he approached a middle-aged woman at the front desk.

"Can I help you?"

"I'm here to see Frank Washington."

"Detective Brown?"

"Yes, ma'am."

She pointed down one of the several hallways leading away from the reception area. "Down there. First door on the right."

"Thank you."

Following her instructions, he entered to find a small waiting area with a few chairs, and one occupied by a lone young girl. A glass wall separated the security chief's office from where the girl sat, and Reggie took a double take when he spotted Frank. The man was a dead ringer for Denzel Washington.

Frank came out of the office. "Detective Brown?"

"Yes." They shook hands. "Reggie is fine."

"Come in."

Frank closed the door behind them and went back around his desk. "The girl you passed on your way in is Caitlin Butler. She's the…" Frank caught the look on his visitor's face. "What?"

Reggie grinned, somewhat embarrassed. "I'm sorry, it's just…"

"I look like Denzel?"

"Yeah!"

"I'd hope so, he's my brother."

"No way!"

Frank laughed. "No, but I do hear it a lot."

"It's uncanny. Anyway, you were saying about the girl in the waiting room."

"Yeah, Caitlin. She's the one who reported Mackenzie missing."

"Does she have any connection to Miss Addison besides the sorority?"

"They are… were roommates."

Reggie looked over his shoulder at the college freshman. Long, curly blonde hair fell around her shoulders, and her tanned skin shimmered beneath a purple tank top and black capris. Worry etched her face, yet it was unlikely she had any idea what Reggie was about to tell her.

He braced himself and let out a sigh. "Let's get this over with."

Frank stood and reopened the door. "Cate?"

She looked up, startled from somewhere deep in thought. "Yes?"

"Would you come in, please?"

Rising on unsteady legs, she moved slowly into the office. Reggie stood to shake her hand. "Hi, Caitlin. My name is Detective Brown."

"Nice to meet you. Did you find Mackenzie?"

Reggie directed her to a chair next to him, waiting until she was seated before answering. "We did, and I'm sorry to say it's not good news."

Tears welled up immediately. "Is she alive?"

Reggie met her gaze directly. "I'm afraid not."

Pain withered the young woman's face as she dissolved into tears. Frank handed her a box of tissues and the two cops allowed the young lady time to gather herself. After several minutes, she did her best to wipe the trail of mascara from her cheeks. "What happened?"

"I'll spare you the details, but she was attacked. When we found her, she was already gone."

"Poor Mackenzie. I need to call her mother."

"That's very good of you, but we'll handle that, okay?"

She bobbed her head once.

"Before we call though, we need to be sure we have a positive ID. Could you help us with that?"

Fear darkened her face. "I don't know. What do I have to do?"

"When you reported Miss Addison missing, you mentioned her having tattoos, is that right?"

"Yes, she had two; a heart and a dolphin."

"Would you know them if you saw them?"

Another bob of her head, this time with more reluctance.

Reggie nodded. "I'd like to show you a couple pictures from the girl we believe is Miss Addison, are you up for that?"

"I guess."

Reggie picked up the tremble in her voice. "Are you okay to do this now?"

She nodded weakly.

The detective opened the folder he had brought with him and slid two pictures out onto the desk. The photos instantly reignited Caitlin's sobs, this time shaking her entire body. She closed her eyes. "Those are hers."

"You're positive?"

Another nod, this time as she looked away from the pictures.

Reggie put the photos back into the file. "Would you like something to drink?"

"Yes, please."

Frank got up and left to fetch a soda. When he returned, he offered her two cans, one a Pepsi, and the other a Diet Coke. She chose the Coke without looking. "Thank you."

"You're welcome."

Reggie had taken out his notepad. After waiting for her to take a few sips, he tested her mindset. "I know this is hard, but do you think you could answer a few questions for me?"

Caitlin wiped at her tears, some of her pain replaced by resolve. "I'll try."

"Great. When was the last time you saw Mackenzie?"

"Sunday night. I was heading home to spend Labor Day with my folks and told her I'd see her on Monday evening."

"And she wasn't there when you got back to the dorm Labor Day night?"

"No. And when she hadn't returned in time for classes Tuesday, I called Brad."

"Brad?"

"Brad Jurgenson. He's Mackenzie's boyfriend."

"What did Brad say when you called?"

"He hadn't seen her since she left his place around seven on Monday night."

"How long had Brad and Mackenzie been going out?"

"Not long; they met at freshman orientation."

"Would you consider their relationship good?"

"Yeah, I think so. She seemed happy."

Reggie made a note. "Can you give me his phone number?"

Caitlin pulled out her cellphone and read it off to the detective.

"Thank you. Do you also have Mackenzie's number?"

She read it off as well.

More scribbling in his notepad. "Can you think of anyone who would want to hurt Mackenzie?"

"Not in a million years. She is... was... such a sweetheart. I can't believe she's gone."

Reggie had pushed hard enough on the girl for now. He closed his pad. "Thank you for your help."

"Of course."

"One thing more, Caitlin."

"Yes?"

"We need time to notify her family, so let's keep Miss Addison's death quiet until then, okay?"

"Sure. I understand."

"Thank you."

Frank escorted her out of the office, spoke with her for a few minutes, then returned to where Reggie sat. "She wanted to know if she could tell *her* mother. I figured she needed someone to comfort her, so I said that would be okay."

Reggie nodded. "That's fine. I'd like to take a look at Mackenzie's dorm room."

"Of course. We can go over there now."

****

The walk across campus to Mackenzie's dorm took several minutes. Along the way, Frank brought Reggie up to date on some other developments.

"When she was first reported missing, we searched Mackenzie's dorm for clues and came up empty. Then, I called Mackenzie's parents to make sure she hadn't gone home."

"Are they local?"

"No, and when they realized I was looking for their daughter, they started the drive into town immediately."

The parents' decision to head for Chicago didn't surprise Reggie at all. He'd do the same thing if he was in their shoes. "When do you expect them?"

"They're coming in from Grand Forks, North Dakota. That's a twelve-hour drive, so sometime this afternoon, maybe."

"Okay. Why don't you have them come down to see me at the precinct?"

"Will do. Are you going to notify them at that time?"

"I can, unless you want to do it first."

An unsettled look crossed the security officer's face. "I've never done a death notification before."

Reggie's expression was haunting. "Unfortunately, I've done too many. I'll handle it for you."

"Thanks."

They walked in silence until Frank turned down a stone path leading up to a large, gothic-like structure. "This is Hammond Hall; Mackenzie and Caitlin shared a room on the third floor."

They climbed the steps, students passing them on both sides in their hurry to get wherever they were going. One face was familiar. Caitlin passed them, a bag in hand, nodding but not slowing down. Reggie gave her a quick smile, and then looked at Frank. "I remember when I could take steps two at a time."

Frank grunted. "Yeah, me too, but I don't have the energy for it these days."

"We're not as young as we used to be, Frank."

"That's seems obvious right now. I guess observations like that are what got you promoted to detective."

Reggie laughed. "Something like that."

On the third floor, Frank knocked at room 312. When no answer came, he tried the door, and found it locked. He produced a master key and unlocked the door. Inside, the blinds were drawn tight and the room dark until Frank flipped on the overhead light.

Reggie stood by the door scanning the room. Having a daughter of his own, the room's state of disarray did not surprise him. Clothes were hung over chairs, make-up was scattered on tables, hair dryers were plugged in and lying on the floor.

Posters took up most of the wall space, with the exception of a photograph over one of the beds. Reggie pulled the photo loose and studied it. Mackenzie, her arm around a good-looking boy, smiled back at the camera. He turned it over.

Brad and me-freshman orientation.

He took a closer look at the boy. He seemed clean-cut, but in the homicide business, looks mean very little. He returned the photo to the wall. "See her phone anywhere?"

"We didn't find it on our first search and I'm not seeing it now. We never found a purse, either."

Reggie took out his own phone and dialed the number given him by Caitlin. Listening to it ring, he hoped Mackenzie's phone would reveal itself nearby, but instead her voicemail picked up. He hung up.

The two men spent a few more minutes leafing through the papers on her desk, looking through her closet, and finally, opening each drawer in her dresser. Eventually, Reggie was satisfied they weren't going to find anything of value and threw up his hands. "Looks as though she hasn't been here since she left to visit her boyfriend."

Frank nodded. "Agreed."

They locked up and left.

Homicide Squad Room
Area 5 Precinct
1:15 pm.

Back at the station, Reggie placed a call to Brad Jurgenson. It went straight to voicemail.

"This is Brad. I'm in class, working, or just ignoring you. Leave a message if you want."

Beep.

"Mr. Jurgenson, my name is Detective Brown with the Chicago PD. Please return my call at this number as soon as possible. Thank you."

He gave his number and hung up.

Next, he wrote a subpoena for Mackenzie Addison's phone records. The girl's iPhone wasn't located in her room, nor at the Zoo Woods crime scene. He dropped the request on the lieutenant's desk just as his phone started to ring.

"Homicide; Detective Brown."

"Reggie, it's Frank Washington."

"Hey, Frank."

"I received a call from Carl and Sharon Addison. Carl estimated he'd be in town by two o'clock."

"Are they coming to the school first?"

"No. I gave them directions to your station and told them to speak with you."

"Did they ask why?"

"Yes. I told them you had taken over the handling of their daughter's disappearance."

"Okay, Frank. Thanks for the heads-up."

"Anytime. If you need anything else, just call."

"Hey, Frank…"

"Yeah?"

"They'll probably want to come over and collect her things. I don't have any problem with that."

54

"Okay, Reggie. Take care."

****

Just past two-thirty, Reggie got a call from the sergeant's desk. "A Carl Addison is asking to see you, Detective."

"I'll be right there."

He found two very anxious people, both looking stressed and weary from a long drive, waiting near the front doors. Reggie's heart went out to them, both for how difficult their trip must have been as they worried about their daughter, and for the news they were yet to learn.

"Mr. and Mrs. Addison?"

"Yes. My name is Carl, this is my wife Sharon."

"Nice to meet you folks. How was your drive down?"

"Very long, Detective. Do you have some news about our daughter?"

Reggie held open the door he'd just come through. "Would you mind following me?"

The Addisons exchanged concerned looks before making their way through the open door. Reggie led them down to the lieutenant's office and asked them to take a seat, before closing the door behind him, and sitting in his boss's chair.

A thick sense of foreboding settled on the room as Reggie looked up to meet their gaze.

"Mr. and Mrs. Addison, there's no easy way to say this... We found your daughter yesterday."

Sharon Addison looked at her husband, then back at the detective. "Where is she?"

"Mrs. Addison, Mackenzie is..."

While Sharon Addison seemed confused, Carl Addison's face already bore the pain of recognition. She stared at the detective blankly, and Carl held up a hand to stop Reggie. "Let me, Detective."

He turned to his wife and took both her hands in his. "Mackenzie is gone, Sweetie."

"Gone? Gone where?"

"She's dead."

The woman's eyes reddened as she looked at Reggie. "Is that true?"

Reggie nodded slowly.

Sharon jerked her hands free from Carl. "There must be some mistake! You must have Mackenzie confused with another girl."

Reggie's voice was barely above a whisper. "I wish I was mistaken, but I'm afraid we've confirmed it was your daughter we found."

Sharon's eyes glazed over, and pain contorted her face. Tears flowed unchecked down her cheeks as she collapsed against her husband, who did his best to comfort her despite his own suffering.

Reggie stood. "I'll give you folks a few minutes."

Outside the office, he closed the door, but you could still hear the sound of their heartbreak coming through. Several detectives looked up at Reggie, a silent nod of their head showing their sympathy and support.

He sat down at his desk, grateful for the distraction when his phone rang. "Detective Brown."

"This is Brad Jurgenson. I had a message to call this number."

"Yes, Brad. I'm investigating the disappearance of your girlfriend, Mackenzie Addison."

"Disappearance? What are you talking about?"

"You didn't know she was missing?"

"No. I got a call from Cate looking for Mackenzie, but I didn't know she was still missing."

"I'm afraid so. Could you come down to the station and talk with me?"

"I guess… when?"

"Right now?"

"Uh… okay. Give me an hour."

"That'll work. Thank you."

Reggie hung up and went back to the lieutenant's office. Inside, the couple had composed themselves somewhat. Carl Addison was still holding his wife. "Can you tell us what happened to our baby girl?"

"The information I have points to an attack sometime on Labor Day. She was found in a city park the next day."

"How… how did she die?"

"I'm afraid she was strangled."

Sharon whimpered. "What... Who...?"

"We don't know yet, but we're doing everything we can to find out."

"I want to see my Mackenzie. Where is she?"

"She's at the Cook County Medical Examiner's Office. I can give you directions, but I need to ask you both a couple questions, if you don't mind."

Carl nodded. "Of course."

"When was the last time you spoke with your daughter?"

"Friday evening. She calls us every Friday to tell us how her week went. Then she calls on Monday night to tell us about her weekend. We never got the Monday call."

"Had Mackenzie ever indicated she was afraid of someone?"

The couple both shook their heads.

"Can you think of anyone who might want to hurt your daughter?"

Again, both shook their heads. Feeling there was nothing more the parents could give him, Reggie slid one of his cards across the desk. "Please call me if you think of anything, okay?"

Carl took the card and stared at it blankly. Sharon sat straight up so abruptly, it startled the detective. "Was Mackenzie raped?"

Surprised, Reggie was instantly grateful for the truth he could give them. "We don't believe so, but I can't say definitively yet."

Sharon stood. "Thank you, detective. I'd like to go see my daughter now."

"Yes, ma'am."

****

Carl and Sharon Addison had been gone just over forty-five minutes when a call came from the front desk. Reggie picked up on the first ring. "Brown."

59

"You have a visitor, Detective."

"Thank you."

In the front lobby, the desk sergeant nodded toward a young, dark-haired boy wearing cargo pants and a Chicago Bears jersey. Reggie extended his hand. "Brad?"

"Yes?"

"I'm Detective Brown."

Brad shook the detective's hand, managing a nervous smile. "Brad Jurgenson."

"Thanks for coming down. Would you follow me?"

Reggie led the boy to an interview room, allowing him to get comfortable. "Would you like a soda or something?"

"No, thanks. I'm fine. Is there any news about Mackenzie?"

Reggie seated himself across a small table from the boy. "I'll get to that in a moment. Is it alright if I ask you a few questions first?"

The detective's refusal to answer ramped up the boy's anxiety. "Uh… sure."

"You said the last time you saw Mackenzie was Monday evening at your home, is that right?"

"Yeah."

"What time did she leave?"

"Around seven."

Reggie had his notepad out. "And you haven't spoken to her since that time?"

"No."

"Why didn't you check on Mackenzie's whereabouts after you received the call from Caitlin Butler?"

"I couldn't."

Reggie raised an eyebrow. "You *couldn't?*"

"Yeah, you see, I'm pledging a fraternity and we were on lockdown going through some qualification drills."

"Hazing?"

"No, definitely not. Just the usual stuff."

"When did it start?"

"Tuesday morning."

"Can your fraternity vouch for you?"

He nodded. "Of course."

"Where were you from the time Mackenzie left Monday night until Tuesday morning?"

"I was studying at my apartment, then sleeping."

"Can anyone verify that?"

"No. I was alone all night."

Reggie made a couple more notes. He didn't get a bad vibe from Brad, but the kid didn't have an alibi. In addition, he's both the boyfriend *and* the last one known to have seen her. Nevertheless, there was no point in keeping the young man in the dark any longer. He closed his notepad. "I have some news about your girlfriend, and I'm afraid it's not good."

Fear took hold and painted itself across the boy's face. "What do you mean by *not good?*"

Reggie sighed. "Mackenzie was found dead on Tuesday."

Brad stared at him, unflinching. Reggie was about to repeat himself when tears traced their way down Brad's face. "Are you sure?"

Reggie nodded.

"What happened?"

"She was murdered."

Brad reacted as if Reggie's words were stuck in his throat, choking him. All the color drained from the young man's face, his eyes rolled back in his head, and he began to slide out of the chair. Reggie caught him before his head hit the floor.

Slapping his cheeks gently at first, then harder, the detective tried to bring the boy around. "Brad! Brad!"

His eyes fluttered open. "Where… What happened?"

Reggie lifted him back into the chair. "You passed out. How do you feel now?"

"Kinda woozy."

Reggie jumped up and left the room, returning quickly with an open can of soda, and set it down in front of Brad. "Take a drink."

The boy sipped the soda, and slowly the color returned to his face. "I'm sorry."

Reggie waved away Brad's concern. "Don't worry about it. It's a shock to anyone when they hear news like that."

The kid's gaze came up to meet the detective's stare. "I would never hurt Mackenzie. You have to believe me!"

"I'm not accusing you of anything, but I do need to know if you and Miss Addison were intimate on Monday."

"You mean like sex?"

Reggie nodded.

Brad averted his eyes and fidgeted in his seat. "Yes."

"You had intercourse on Monday?"

"Yes. What does that matter?"

Reggie softened his tone. "You have to trust me, Brad. It's important."

"Fine. Are we done?"

"Yes, but I would like to get a DNA swab from you."

"Whatever. Just do it and let me get out of here."

As soon as Reggie finished getting the sample, Brad stood. "Can I leave?"

"Yes, and thank you for your cooperation."

Brad nodded before disappearing through the open door. Reggie rubbed his temples, his head now serving as an anvil for an imaginary hammer. He asked himself the same question.

Can I leave?

When he got back to his desk and found nothing needing his immediate attention, he answered his own question by heading for the door.

*Home of
Sonya & Reggie Brown
Eastside Neighborhood
6:45 p.m.*

After dinner, Reggie plopped on the couch with a glass of wine and turned on the TV. Sonya finished cleaning up the kitchen and came into the living room, standing behind her husband. Slowly, she massaged his shoulders. "A bad one today, Reggie?"

"One of the worst."

"Do you want to talk about it?"

"Yes and no. It's not the case itself, but I did something today I've never had to do in thirty years."

She pressed her knuckles into his back. "Oh?"

"If you can imagine, I had to do no less than three death notifications today."

"Three?"

"Three. Every time is agonizing, you know that from watching me, but three in one day was unbelievably difficult."

She closed her eyes in an attempt to block the vision. "I don't know how you do it, Reggie. I couldn't imagine going through it even once, never mind three times in one day."

She worked her fingers around his neck, finally beginning to feel a little easing of his tension, when her palm came away wet. "What's this?"

He looked over his shoulder. "Oh, is that bleeding again?"

Sonya pulled down his shirt collar to get a better look. "How long have you had this?"

He shrugged. "A while."

"Has it always bled like this?"

"No. Today was the first time I've noticed any blood."

She left the room and returned promptly with a damp tissue to dab at the spot. "I don't like it, Reggie. You should have it looked at."

He waved a hand in the air. "It's nothing. I'll have it looked at after I'm retired."

Sonya moved around in front of him, standing between him and the TV. Placing both hands on her hips, she glared at him. "Let me rephrase my statement; you *will* have that looked at!"

Her eyes told him there was no point in arguing with her. He'd fought this fire too many times before. He sighed. "Fine. You make the appointment; I'll go. Deal?"

She smiled and planted a kiss on his forehead. "Deal."

"Good. Now, get yourself a glass of wine, sit your hind end on this couch, and snuggle up next to me."

Thursday, September 4

Homicide Squad Room
Area 5 Precinct
8:15 a.m.

Like most people her age, Mackenzie Addison spent a lot of time on the phone, evidenced by the size of the paper pile waiting for him the next morning, that was made up of the girl's phone records. With a full coffee mug, he sat down and began the task of sorting out his victim's electronic life.

The first page contained the last pings on Mackenzie's phone and the result of the test ping his subpoena had requested. The test ping had come up empty. The final recorded ping on her phone bounced off a tower near Zoo Woods, where her body was dumped.

Reggie rubbed his forehead. *That phone is probably at the bottom of the river!*

He flipped to the second page, uncapped a yellow highlighter, and started in on a line-by-line review.

Three hours and as many cups of coffee later, he turned over the last page. Despite being a talkative girl, Mackenzie proved to have a fairly small circle of friends. He had found nothing out of the ordinary.

No unexplained phone numbers.

No threatening text messages.

No unusual communication at all.

"Nothing!"

"What was that, Reggie?"

Reggie turned to find Lieutenant Davis looking over his shoulder. "Oh, hi Jerry. I just finished with the victim's phone records and came up empty."

"Have you got anything else to go on?"

"Not much. I'm waiting for the DNA results, but that's about it. Neither the roommate nor the boyfriend was much help. The parents are in from out of town but they knew very little about their daughter's day-to-day life."

"Keep at it."

"Yes, sir." Reggie's phone range. "Detective Brown; Homicide."

"Hey, Reggie. It's me."

"Hi, Babe. What's up?"

"You have an appointment at the doctor's."

He'd almost forgotten his pledge from the night before. "Today?"

"Yes, today!"

Most folks had to wait a week, but not Sonya. She held a secret power not shared by most folks.

"I'm kinda busy."

"Reginald Brown, you promised!"

She had him dead to rights. "What time?"

"One-thirty."

He looked at his watch. "I'll be there."

"Good. Love you, bye."

He hung up. In truth, with no new leads to chase, he wasn't busy at all. He checked his watch again.

Just enough time for lunch at B & B before the appointment.

Batter and Berries
North Lincoln Ave.
12:30 p.m.

A new yellow awning hung over the entrance on North Lincoln, announcing breakfast, brunch, and lunch. The bright color continued inside the small storefront to the walls. The tables were packed a little close together, but ever since it opened in 2012, Batter and Berries had become his favorite place to eat.

His waitress set a large plate of pancakes in front of him. "Here you go, Reggie. Enjoy."

"Thanks, Marie."

"Get you a refill on your coffee?"

"Please."

Spreading butter over the stack, he liberally applied syrup before digging in. The thirty-minute drive from the precinct was a small price to pay for the delicious treat. Besides, today it put him just five minutes from the doctor's office.

The first bite was on its way to his mouth when his phone rang. He contemplated stuffing the food in, but it would take him too long to chew it before he could answer. He set the still full fork back on the plate and answered the call.

"This is Detective Brown."

"Hi, Reggie. Janet Thorsen."

"Hey, Janet. You better have good news because you're interrupting my favorite lunch."

She laughed. "What's that?"

"Pancakes at Batter and Berries."

"Oh, I love that place!"

"My stack is getting cold, Janet."

She laughed again. "Okay, okay. I've got DNA results for you. The semen sample from Miss Addison was a match to her boyfriend, Brad Jurgenson, and there was no other DNA mixed with his."

"Okay, what about the fingernail cuttings?"

"We got a strong profile, and it wasn't the boyfriend's. Unfortunately, the CODIS search came back without a match."

"Super! Would you send me a copy of the report?"

"It'll be on your desk. Enjoy your lunch."

"I will. Bye."

Reggie lifted the fork and savored the first bite. Even the DNA results couldn't wipe the smile from his face.

****

A slight breeze pushed the comfortable September air against his face as he walked the six blocks to the doctor's office. He made it through the door with five minutes to spare. Sonya and he had been going to Lincoln Park Clinic for over twenty-years, and Doctor Tim was as much a friend as their physician. Tall, lean, and handsome, the fifty-something doctor was perpetually in a good mood. "Reggie, good to see you."

"Hey, Tim. How's things?"

"Good as ever." He dropped onto a rolling stool and opened the chart in his hands. "Now, what is it that brings you in?"

"Sonya, of course. She's worried about this spot on my neck."

"Okay, let's take a look." The physician squinted at the spot Reggie indicated. "Remove your shirt, will ya?"

Reggie complied and the doc's fingers probed around the spot, then moved to several other locations on his back, all while not speaking. After several minutes, he returned to the stool. "You can put your shirt back on, Reggie."

When he was re-dressed, the doctor looked up from his chart and his smile was gone. "I'm glad Sonya sent you in. That spot and a couple others are very concerning."

"Concerning in what way?"

"Well, let me start by saying I don't want to scare you."

Reggie smiled. "Okay Doc, but you're stalling is beginning to scare me."

Tim's smile returned with a laugh. "Fair enough. I want you to have a dermatologist look at these and see if they need biopsied."

"You're worried about cancer?"

"I am, but I'm not the one to say, and there are three kinds of skin cancer; two of which are not serious when caught early."

"Okay. When do I go?"

"I'll have my assistant, Kimberly, make the appointment, and let you know."

"I'm on a case right now, so have her call Sonya."

The doctor stood and extended his hand. "That'll be fine."

"Thanks again, Tim."

"No problem. Good to see you again, Reggie."

"Likewise."

****

Reggie waited until he got back to his car before he called Sonya. She was going to go off the deep end when he mentioned the "C" word.

"Hello?"

"Hey, Sweetie."

"Hi. What did Tim say?"

"He's sending me to a dermatologist."

"Why?"

"He wants a specialist's opinion."

"What did he think it was?"

Reggie took a deep breath. "He's not sure, but he wants to rule out skin cancer."

"Cancer! Oh, Reggie. What'll we do?"

He smiled to himself. "I'm not dying, Sonya. Tim said even if it is cancer, two of the three types are not serious."

"When do you go to the specialist?"

"His assistant is going to call you with the appointment."

"Okay…"

He sensed she was near tears. "Sonya?"

"Yes?"

"It's going to be fine. Tim isn't even sure if it is cancer, so let's not be too worried before it's necessary, okay?"

"Okay."

"I need to get back to work. Love you."

"I love you, too."

Reggie hung up, started the car, and headed for the precinct. He was grateful to have the case as a distraction.

Production Meeting Room
WWND-10 Studios
North Center
3:45 p.m.

Chad followed Vince out of the production meeting and down to his office. They were just over an hour away from the early edition of the evening news and they had some copy to go over. Chad looked at his cell phone. He had a voicemail.

As Chad listened, Vince picked up on the stiffening of his body. "What is it?"

"It's him!"

"Him, who?"

"The killer who left the voicemail about Mackenzie Addison."

"Are you sure?"

"Yes, I'm sure! It's the same electronic sound disguising his words."

"What did he say?"

"Listen."

Vince grabbed his reporter by the arm and steered him into his office. Shutting the door before turning to Chad. "Put it on speaker."

Chad hit the button and the message filled the room.

"*I've selected my next victim. Her time is nearly here. She will die as Mackenzie did.*"

They stared at each other as Chad played it again. When it was done, Chad dialed a number.

"What are you doing?"

Chad looked up in surprise. "Calling Detective Brown, why?"

"Hold off on that for a minute."

"Why?"

"Let's think about this."

Chad was still holding the receiver. "What are you talking about? Brown needs to know about this; another girl's life is in danger."

Vince was pacing now. "I know, I know. But we've got an hour until early edition, and no one has this scoop but us. Why take the risk of someone else finding out? We can call the detective just before we go on the air."

Chad just stared at him. "Are you hearing yourself? You're talking about hindering an investigation, maybe even concealing evidence."

Vince turned on him. "Oh, come on! Information releases are stalled and delayed all the time in the name of getting the story."

"Not when it has to do with people's lives!"

Vince held his ground. "Look, just give me ten minutes to consult with Reilly."

Chad set the receiver down. "Fine. Ten minutes, and not a second longer."

"Good."

Homicide Squad Room
Area 5 Precinct
4:00 p.m.

Reggie sat at his desk reviewing the DNA report sent by the coroner. It wasn't that he thought he might see something Janet didn't mention, but more because he didn't have another direction to go. He closed the folder and leaned back in his chair.

Staring at the ceiling, he let the three issues most concerning him make their way through his mind, where they combined to force his blood pressure to rise. The case, which had stalled and was already threatening to go cold. The possibility he had cancer, and the pending appointment with the specialist. And the last but not least, the idea of retiring with his last case unsolved.

The burst of noise as his desk phone rang pulled him out of his misery. "Homicide; Brown."

"Detective, this is Chad Marshall."

"Yes, Chad. What can I do for you?"

"I've got another message."

Reggie's pulse shot up. "The same guy?"

"It sounds like it to me."

"Did he give you a location of another body?"

"No, this was a warning. Do you want to hear it?"

"Where are you?"

"At the studios."

"Do you know where Kilbourn Park is?"

"Sure."

"There's a bench just inside the entrance. Can you meet me there?"

"That's fine. Fifteen minutes?"

Reggie checked his watch. "Perfect, and bring me a copy of the message."

"Will do."

Kilbourn Park
North Side
4:35 p.m.

Reggie waited impatiently, watching the leaves rustling in the on again, off again breeze. He spotted the news van coming to a stop just yards away, and Chad Marshall was quickly out and approaching him, his gait purposeful. He stood to greet the reporter. "Thanks for meeting me, Chad."

"No problem. You want to hear it?"

"Please."

Chad played it back.

Reggie listened to it twice. "Did you bring me a copy?"

Chad reached into his back pocket and pulled out a flash drive. "Yeah; here."

"How about the phone number of the caller."

Chad handed him a piece of paper. "I need to get back. Is there anything else?"

"No, and thanks Chad."

Office of
Lieutenant Jerry Davis
Area 5 Precinct
5:10 p.m.

Reggie tapped on his lieutenant's door. "Got a minute, Jerry?"

Davis looked up from some paperwork. "Of course. Come in."

"I just came from meeting Chad Marshall. He received another message."

"From the same person?"

"Yeah. You want to listen to it?"

"Indeed." Davis laced his fingers together in front of his face and closed his eyes. When the playback ended, he sighed. "Crap!"

Reggie shrugged. "I'm not sure what to do. We can't warn every campus in the city."

"No, and besides, he didn't indicate the girl was from a college campus. He might attempt to take his next victim from anywhere in the city."

Reggie leaned back, focusing on the ceiling above him, as if looking for divine guidance. "But if we do nothing, we can be accused of failing to warn the public."

Jerry shook his head. "There's nothing to warn them about. We don't know if it's tonight or tomorrow, maybe even next week. Secondly, if we did say something, we're likely to give every nut with a gun an excuse to shoot first and ask questions later."

His boss was right, of course. "What about Frank Washington at CCC? Should we let him know?"

Davis thought about it, then shook his head. "We have nothing indicating the killer will return to the same campus, if he goes back to a college at all. No, we just have to wait it out and hope Chad gets another message."

Reggie didn't like it, but he had to agree. "Here's the number Chad gave me from his voicemail."

"I'll request the records immediately."

Standing up, Reggie stretched his big frame toward the ceiling. "In that case, I'm gonna call it a day. See you tomorrow, Jerry."

Home of
Sonya & Reggie Brown
Eastside Neighborhood
6:10 p.m.

That night, Reggie and Sonya sat together in silence. She had worn an unchanging frown since he arrived home, her worry about his biopsy overruling her delight at seeing him get home early.

She sipped her wine. "Your appointment is at eight with a Dr. Scott."

"Where?"

"Same building as Tim; office number 505."

"Okay."

A familiar voice from the TV news intruded on their conversation. Chad Marshall's face filled their TV screen.

"That's right, Mark. The investigation continues into the death of Mackenzie Addison, but in the meantime, this reporter has received another exclusive communication from the presumed killer."

Film of the Zoo Woods crime scene played back as the reporter spoke. When the live shot returned to him, Chad held up his phone to the camera.

"While I cannot reveal the exact content of the message, the caller indicated he's not done killing. Though his voice was disguised, his meaning was clear—there will be more victims if he isn't caught."

Reggie groaned. "What is he trying to do, start a panic?" He turned the TV off. "He can't start telling everyone the killer isn't done!"

He went to rub his neck, but stopped when he remembered he was told to leave the spot alone. He ran his hands through his hair instead. "The public is gonna want answers we can't give them."

Sonya snuggled up to her husband. "Forget about it. The public can wait until tomorrow to *not* get their answers. Tonight, you're with me."

He forced himself to calm down, then kissed her forehead. "The place I'm happiest, that's for sure."

CCC Campus Housing
Norwood Park
11:30 p.m.

Gina Montrose stepped out of the breezeway and onto the lawn behind the dorm building, letting the wind catch her long, auburn hair. Lighting up, she took a deep drag on the cigarette and soaked in the quiet. These late night smoke breaks from her studies had become a regular part of her routine and as she leaned against the back of the building, her proximity to the bushes didn't concern her.

It should have.

She let her guard down for just a moment, and as the wire tightened around her throat, she realized it was a fatal error.

Friday, September 5

Apartment of Chad Marshall
Balmoral Ave
7:45 a.m.

Chad stepped out of the hot shower and toweled himself off. Not due at the station until eight-thirty, he'd slept in, then indulged with an extra cup of coffee. He'd been up late the night before doing a live report on the eleven o'clock news, and Reilly had released him from the morning production meeting.

Wrapping a towel around himself, he went into the bedroom to dress. His phone was lying on his bedside table and it was flashing. He scooped it up and stared at the notification. Another voicemail.

Office of Doctor James Scott
Lincoln Park Clinic
8:20 a.m.

Reggie sat on the examination bed, his shirt off, and tried to understand how the doctor could be running behind schedule already. *Aren't I the first appointment of the day?*

Five minutes later, the door opened. A man nearly half Reggie's size, in both height and weight, came into the room. Dr. James Scott was embroidered over the chest pocket of his lab coat. "Good morning… Reggie, is it?"

"Yeah."

"I'm Jim Scott." Despite his diminutive size, the doctor possessed a strong handshake. "Let's get you to lie down on your stomach and I'll take a closer look."

Reggie turned over and stretched out, his feet dangling precariously off the bed, as the doctor donned a set of goggles that looked like he found them on a sci-fi movie set. They appeared part illuminator, part microscope, and the doctor's eyes took on a grotesque shape through the lenses.

Flipping on the headset's lights, he probed Reggie's back in several areas, spending extra time at the spot on his neck. He didn't speak during the exam, but after turning to a surgical tray, he rotated back to Reggie holding a scalpel. "I'm going to take a biopsy of this growth on the neck, Reggie. You'll feel a little scraping."

Reggie didn't bother to answer, and shortly, he felt the sharp instrument digging into his skin. The scalpel had just lifted from his neck when a phone started ringing in the corner. It took a second for the detective to realize it was his. "Sorry, Doc. I forgot to shut it off."

"That's fine. Let me get a bandage on your neck and you can answer it."

By the time Reggie pulled his phone out of his jacket, the caller had hung up. Reggie noted it was from the lieutenant before shutting off the phone.

The doctor was putting the biopsy sample into a glass tube and labeling it. "You can put your shirt back on, Reggie."

While Reggie dressed, Dr. Scott made some notes, then turned back to his patient. "I'm going to send this away for analysis. It will probably be a couple days until it comes back, and we'll call you with the results."

"What do you think, Doc?"

"I don't like to predict test results, but I *am* concerned about it. The other spots don't have the same indications as the neck growth, so I didn't biopsy them, but the spot on your neck does show troubling signs."

Reggie shrugged. "You're the doctor."

Jim Scott looked down at his chest pocket. "Well, I have the lab coat anyway."

Reggie laughed. "Hopefully, that's not all!"

"Indeed. Do you have any questions?"

Reggie shook his head. "Not really."

"Okay, then. You don't need to stop at the desk; just head out."

"Thanks, Doc."

Back out in the parking lot, Reggie dialed his lieutenant, who answered on the first ring. "Homicide; Lieutenant Davis."

"Jerry, it's me."

"Reggie, are you done at the doctor's?"

"Yeah, just finished. What's up?"

"Your reporter friend got another call."

"Another warning?"

"Another body."

Salt Creek Bridge
3 Miles West of Zoo Woods
9:30 a.m.

Reggie arrived at the scene to find the van from WWND-10 already set up and Chad was testing his microphone.

"Hey, Detective."

"Hi, Chad. I'll need a copy of that message."

"I've got it right here. It sounds exactly like the rest of them."

"I figured." Reggie accepted the flash drive, which had a piece of paper taped to it. "What's this?"

"The number that left the message."

"Great; thanks."

"So Detective, can you give us any information about the victim?"

"Did you look over the scene before the responding officers arrived?"

"Yes."

Reggie scowled. "Did you touch anything?"

"No, of course not."

"Look Chad, you need to leave my crime scenes alone! I can't have you contaminating my evidence, not to mention giving a defense attorney plenty to call into question, do you understand?"

"Yeah, sure. I only looked down from the bridge at the scene."

Reggie snorted. "In that case, I imagine you know more than I do." He stomped off in the direction of the crime tape.

At least five different locations around the Salt Creek *Woods* allowed access to the Salt Creek *Trail*. One of those entrances was in the upscale residential neighborhood where they stood, where a trail led to the Salt Creek *Bridge,* which crossed Salt *Creek*.

Just keeping it straight was already giving Reggie a headache.

Less than fifty yards into the thick woods, he found the responding officer leaning against the bridge railing, watching what was going on below. Ducking under the crime tape, the detective approached with his badge held out. "What have we got?"

The officer straightened up. "Single female, early twenties, apparently strangled."

"Were you first on the scene?"

"Yes, sir. I made my way down to where she was and checked for a pulse, but she was cold."

Reggie looked over the side of the rusted steel bridge, scanning the overall layout of the area. September had been dry so far this year, and the creek was low, exposing the clay banks beneath the overhanging trees. This was where the body had been dumped, but any more detail was blocked from view by the forensic techs working around her.

Reggie turned back to the officer. "Let's get a canvas started of the homes along Jackson and Brainerd streets."

"Yes, sir."

Retracing his steps to the end of the bridge, Reggie followed the broken trail down to the girl's body. It was eerily familiar to the Mackenzie Addison scene.

The girl was on her back, her head barely in the water, her long red hair being tugged by the current. A baggy t-shirt was wrapped around her torso, her shoes were gone, and her sweatpants were at her ankles. There was no sign of her underwear.

An officer came around the body and up to the detective. "Victim's name is Gina Montrose."

"How did you ID her?"

"We found this."

Reggie took the baggie offered him and held it up to the sky. He was looking at an identification badge from the Central College of Chicago. "Crap."

"Detective Brown, we meet again."

Reggie looked up to see Janet Thorsen working her way down the embankment. He smiled. "Nice to see you, Doc. Are you following me?"

"No."

He let his smile drop, giving up his quest for the moment. "Looks similar to the Zoo Woods scene."

Janet bent over the body, touching the girl's neck. "At first glance, the weapon appears the same."

Reggie made a note, and when he looked back at the body, Janet had Miss Montrose's mouth pried open and was holding something out to him. "You got an evidence bag handy?"

"What's that?"

"Looks like a pledge pin to me."

Reggie held out a bag and she dropped it in. "Did you find it…?"

"In her mouth. Yes."

Reggie held the bag up to the sky. Though he'd studied the Greek letters in looking up the first victim's sorority, his memory wasn't good enough to remember the letters on this pin. It would have to wait until he got back to the precinct.

One thing was certain; the phone messages to the reporter weren't the only things tying these cases together. The signatures were identical; he had a serial killer on his hands.

I should have retired sooner.

Making his way back to his car, he dropped into the front seat and pulled out his phone. He found the number he was looking for in his call history and dialed.

"College Security; this is Washington."

"Frank, this is Reggie Brown."

"Hey, Detective. Is there any news?"

"Not on the Addison case, I'm afraid."

"Too bad."

"Actually, I'm calling about another student at your school."

An uneasiness crept into Frank's voice. "Oh?"

"Do you have any new reports of a missing girl?"

"No… not that I'm aware of. What are you getting at?"

"I need you to write down a name and check on something for me."

"Okay. What's the name?"

"Gina… Montrose. Got that?"

"Sure. What do you need to know?"

Reggie hesitated. "Well… I've got another body, Frank."

"Another?"

"I'm afraid so, and I believe the name I just gave you is our victim."

Frank's unease had turned to shock. "Son of a... I'll get right on it and call you back."

"Frank?"

"Yeah?"

"Be discreet, okay?"

"Of course."

Reggie sighed. "Thanks."

He closed his phone and his eyes.

I'm getting too old for this. Of course you are, dummy. That's why you're retiring!

A knock on his window startled him. "Detective?"

The officer from the bridge was now standing next to his car door. Reggie rolled down his window. "What's up?"

"I've got a lady who thinks she may have seen something."

Adrenaline surged through Reggie, perking him up immediately. "Really?"

"Yes. I told her you would want to speak to her."

Reggie climbed out of his car. "Where is she?"

"Follow me."

Reggie trailed the officer up Jackson Avenue, and just three houses from the trail entrance, they turned up the walkway of a small home. White clapboard siding, with gray shutters and gray shingles, the outside of the little home was immaculate. Sitting on the tiny front veranda, sliding back and forth on a metal porch glider, was a woman in her mid-seventies. A yellow smock hung loosely around her petite frame, and her hair, matching the gray of her homes trim, was pulled up in a bun.

"Mrs. Esposito, this is the detective I told you about. His name is Detective Brown."

Reggie stepped over as the officer retreated. "Nice to meet you, ma'am."

"Likewise, Detective Brown. Would you like to pull up a chair?"

Reggie sat on a bench across from her. "Thank you. Please call me Reggie."

"Okay, Reggie. You can call me Stella."

Reggie smiled. "Nice to meet you, Stella."

"Likewise, Reggie."

He took out his notepad. "The officer said you may have seen something interesting last night?"

"That's right. When you get to be my age, you don't tend to sleep very well. When I'm up this time of year, I like to come out on the porch for the breeze. Usually, I'll relax enough so I can go back to sleep."

Reggie nodded. "I imagine it's quite peaceful."

"In fact, it usually is, but not last night."

"What was different about last night?"

"Well, when I came out on the porch, there was a car down there at the entrance to the trail…"

"What time was this?"

"About twelve-thirty or so. Anyway, as I was sayin', this car was down there with its lights off. I see this man get out and open the trunk…"

"How did you determine it was a man?"

Stella stopped her gliding and fixed the detective with a stern glare. "Reggie, didn't your mama teach you not to interrupt folks when they're speakin'?"

Reggie grinned at her. "Yes ma'am, she most certainly did. I apologize and it won't happen again."

Stella smirked at him, a twinkle in her eyes. "See to it that it doesn't!"

"I will."

She resumed her back and forth gliding.

"So… when this *man* opened the trunk, an inside light came on. That's when I saw *him*." She sipped her drink. "Would you like some iced tea, Reggie?"

"No, thank you, ma'am."

"Very well. Where was I? Oh yes… he lifted something heavy onto his shoulder, *slammed* the trunk, and went off into the trail entrance. A few minutes later, he returned, got in his car, and *slammed* the door again. It was very loud."

Reggie paused, unsure if she was done. She smiled at him. "You can ask your questions now, Reggie."

He laughed. He felt comfortable with her, in large part because she reminded him of his own mother. "Can you describe the car, Stella?"

"Oh, I'm afraid I'm not much good on cars. Dark colored, medium size, four doors, I think."

Reggie made the notations. "What about him? Anything you can tell me about him?"

"Well, my eyes aren't great, but I did see he was colored."

"I'm sorry?"

"Oh, I don't mean to be rude, Reggie. I mean, he was dark-skinned; black or maybe Hispanic."

"I see. What was he wearing?"

"Jeans and one of those hoodsy things, I think."

"A hoodie?"

"Yeah, that's it."

97

"Could you tell the color of the hoodie?"

"Dark, maybe blue or black."

Reggie stood. "Stella, it's been a pleasure to meet you." He handed her a business card. "If you think of anything else, will you call me?"

"Of course. Are you sure you wouldn't like some tea?"

"I've got to run, but can I get a rain check?"

She smiled up at him, the same twinkle in her eyes. "I suppose that would be just fine."

Homicide Squad Room
Area 5 Precinct
1:00 p.m.

Reggie had driven through a burger joint on the way back to the precinct, and was chomping some fries as he went over the sorority list at his desk. He'd identified the pin found at the second crime scene as belonging to Kappa Gamma Phi.

His phone rang, forcing him to swallow quickly. "Homicide; Brown."

"Detective, it's Frank Washington."

"Yeah, Frank."

"I can confirm that Gina Montrose's roommate hasn't seen her since last night. I checked with her professors and she missed all her classes today."

"Have you contacted her family, yet?"

"No. I was waiting to talk to you."

"You'd better call. We need to be certain she isn't with them, and if she isn't, we need them come to the morgue for identification. Where do they live?"

"Gary, Indiana."

"Okay. That's just a forty-five-minute drive or so, right?"

"Yeah, about that."

"Frank… do you want me to call them?"

"No, I'll handle it, but thanks."

"Let me know what you find out."

"Will do."

The line went dead and Reggie hung up. He gathered the remainder of his fries and pitched them in the trash. His appetite had deserted him.

Something had been tugging at the back of his mind, and he'd finally figured out what it was. He dialed Chad Marshall's number.

"Hello?"

"Chad, this is Reggie Brown."

"Hi, Detective. What can I do for you?"

"Are you tied up right now?"

"I'm on my way back to the station. We just got done with a midday live report from Salt Creek."

"Would you mind coming by the station and talking to me?"

"No… I guess not. Will it take long?"

"Probably not. I just have a few questions."

"Okay. I'll be there shortly."

"Thanks."

The phone was still in Reggie's hand when another line lit up with a new call. He punched the button. "Homicide; Brown."

"Reggie, this is Frank. I got hold of Mr. and Mrs. Montrose. They hadn't heard from their daughter in a few days."

"Did you fill them in?"

"I did. I told them she was missing and they needed to come to the college. I figured it was best to tell them the rest in person."

"You're probably right. Let me know when they arrive."

"Will do."

Interview Room
Area 5 Precinct
1:45 p.m.

Reggie pointed toward a chair on one side of a small table, closed the door, and then sat down on the opposite side. He laid his notepad on the desk and looked up at the reporter. "Thanks for coming in, Chad."

"Sure. Why did you need to talk to me?"

"Well, frankly, I wouldn't be doing my job if I didn't take an official statement from you."

"About the murders?"

"Yes, about the murders."

Chad couldn't hide his surprise. "You're kidding, right?"

Reggie smiled. "Don't take offense, it's just protocol. After all, you're the one who knew about both murders before anyone else. I would interview anyone in your situation."

Chad relaxed slightly. "Well, I guess if you put it that way."

Reggie clicked his pen. "Right, so where were you the night of September first?"

"Let's see, that was Labor Day and I was off, so Christie and I took a drive. We stopped for lunch at Fox Lake, and then came home for a quiet dinner. We turned in about ten, I think."

"Christie is your girlfriend?"

"Yeah, we live together."

"What's her last name?"

"Shaw, Christie Shaw."

Reggie jotted it down. "And she can confirm your account of the day and night?"

"Of course."

"Okay, now what about Thursday the fourth?"

"I worked all day, mostly on the Addison case, including meeting you at Kilbourn Park."

Reggie grinned. "I guess *I* can verify that part of your story."

Chad smiled. "I appreciate that! Anyway, after doing the late news, I went home and stayed in with Christie."

"And she can verify you were there all night?"

"Yeah, sure."

"How can I get in touch with her?"

"She works at the Shriner's Hospital for Children."

Reggie closed his notebook. "That'll be all for now. Thanks again for coming in, and for how much help you've been."

"You're welcome." Chad looked at his watch. "I need to beat it for the station. See ya."

Security Offices
Central College of Chicago
Norwood Park
3:00 p.m.

Reggie had left his meeting with Chad and driven over to CCC, even though he hadn't heard from Frank about the Montroses yet. He found Frank standing by the front desk at the security office.

"Hey, Detective. The parents haven't arrived yet."

"That's fine. I was hoping to check out Miss Montrose's room and talk to her roommate."

"Sure." Frank turned to the receptionist. "Call me on the radio when Mr. and Mrs. Montrose get here."

"Yes, sir."

Frank went into his office and returned shortly with some keys. "Come with me, Reggie."

Gina's sorority house appeared deserted when they arrived a few minutes later. Reggie gave an inquisitive look to the security chief. "Where is everybody?"

"Pep rally. The football team has their home opener tomorrow."

"Oh. I was afraid word had gotten out and everyone was gone."

A wry smile crossed Frank's face. "Not yet."

Gina's room was on the first floor, and like the rest of the hall, empty. The inside was much like Mackenzie's: messy, disorganized, and lived-in. They had just started to look around when a girl appeared at the door. "Can I help you?"

As the officers turned, she recognized Frank. "Oh, hi Officer Washington. Any word on Gina?"

The two men exchanged quick looks, Reggie shaking his head slightly. Frank smiled at the girl. "Not yet, Tammy. Is the rally over?"

"No, I just wasn't in the mood. I'm too worried about Gina."

"That's understandable. Tammy Williams, this is Detective Brown. He's helping with the search for Gina."

Tammy nodded at the detective. "Hi."

Reggie smiled. "Hello. Do you mind answering a few questions?"

"No, of course not."

Reggie took out his notepad. "When was the last time you saw your friend?"

"Around midnight; she went out for a smoke."

"Is it common for her to go out that late for a smoke?"

"Yeah. She likes to study late and will take a smoke break every so often."

"Is there a smoking room in the building?"

"Yes, but she doesn't use it. Most of the time, she steps off the back of the breezeway."

Reggie raised an eyebrow. "Breezeway? Can you show me where that is?"

"Sure."

Before the girl could lead them out the door, Reggie stopped her. "Tammy?"

"Yeah?"

"Did Gina have her phone with her?"

"No." She pointed across the room. "It's lying on the shelf over there."

Reggie pulled a handkerchief from his pocket and lifted the phone into an evidence bag, then looked up at the girl. "Can you show me where that breezeway is now?"

Her brow furrowed with concern as she watched how Reggie handled the phone. "Sure… okay."

Following her out of the room and down the hall, they exited a side door that led out into a covered outdoor portico. Across the way was the other half of the dormitory building. The name was fitting, as the wind blew through the hall with significant force. Tammy turned right and stepped out onto the back lawn, then pointed. "She usually stood right there."

Reggie examined the spot carefully. Lying on the ground was a cigarette butt. "Tammy, do you know what brand of cigarette she smoked?"

"Sure. Capris."

Reggie put on a glove and gathered the butt into an evidence bag, studying it first. He could barely make out the letters 'C A' running along what remained of the cigarette.

The radio on Frank's hip crackled to life. "Frank, you copy?"

"Yeah, go for Frank."

"Mr. and Mrs. Montrose are here."

"Copy that. Ask them to sit in my office and I'll be there in a minute."

"Yes, sir."

Tammy's eyes grew wide and her face flushed. "Gina's parents are here?"

Frank nodded. "It's normal to let them know when there is concern for a child."

Suspicion took over Tammy's expression. "There's more you aren't telling me, isn't there?"

Frank and Reggie exchanged looks. Reggie took the lead. "Frank, you go and meet with Gina's parents while I have a talk with Tammy."

Frank nodded. "Okay. Do you want to meet me back at the office?"

"Yeah, I'll be along in a few."

As Frank was leaving, Reggie spotted a bench across the lawn. "Tammy, let's sit over there and talk for a few minutes, okay?"

The girl suddenly looked very small, and her eyes welled up with tears as she followed the detective to the bench. When they were seated, he looked directly into her eyes and saw the fear. "Tammy, we believe your friend may have been harmed."

Tammy started to shake and tears rolled down her cheeks. Reggie dug out a handkerchief and gave it to her.

"Is she… is she dead?"

"We aren't certain, but it looks that way."

Tammy began to sob, and leaned against the big detective. He pulled her close and waited. It reminded him of all the times his daughter had suffered some insult or a broken heart, and leaned on him for comfort. It hurt him then and it hurt him now.

After several minutes, Tammy forced herself to sit up. She'd stopped sobbing, but her face bore the evidence of her tears. Reggie still had questions, and sensing she was calm enough for a few, he took out his notepad.

"Tammy, can you answer a few more questions?"

She nodded.

"Did Gina have a boyfriend?"

"No."

"A love interest of any kind?"

She shook her head. "She'd had a long relationship with a guy at home, but when they went off to different colleges, they ended it."

"Did she say it was amicable?"

"Yeah, at least I think so. She never said otherwise."

"What about anyone else? Did anyone seem unusually interested in her? Was she bothered by anyone in her classes?"

Another shake of the head. "Not that I know of. We had talked about how creepy it was that a guy was hanging around the sorority houses, but we weren't sure if it was just a story or not. We never actually saw him."

Reggie raised an eyebrow. "What do you know about this guy?"

She shrugged. "Not much. We heard some of the girls talking about an incident at another sorority house."

Reggie made a note to ask Frank about the rumor. "One last thing, Tammy. I need you to remain quiet about all this."

"Why?"

"Well, because nothing is confirmed yet. We don't want to get ahead of ourselves, okay?"

"Okay."

Reggie stood. "I need to make a call. Will you be alright?"

"Yeah. Can I go to my dorm?"

"Yes, but please stay on your side of the room, okay?"

"Okay."

Reggie watched her walk away, then returned to the spot where he'd found the cigarette butt. Less than four feet away was a thick clump of bushes. Walking around to the far side, he found a disturbed area of soil, at least part of which contained a shoe impression. Taking his phone out, he dialed the lieutenant.

"This is Lieutenant Davis."

"Jerry, it's Reggie. I need a forensic team out at Central College."

"What have you got?"

"I think I've found the spot where victim two was attacked."

"I'll send one immediately."

"And Jerry?"

"Yeah?"

"Tell them to keep it low-key."

"Will do."

Reggie closed his cell phone. He would have to stand guard until the techs arrived.

I wonder how Frank is doing.

Security Offices
Central College of Chicago
Norwood Park
4:15 p.m.

After directing the forensic team to the area on the back lawn, and transferring the cigarette butt to their possession, he asked that a plaster cast be made of the shoe impression. Reggie then made his way back to the campus security office and into the waiting area outside of Frank's office, where an older couple he assumed was Mr. and Mrs. Montrose, sat with Washington.

Frank spotted him and waved the detective in.

Both people looked up when Reggie entered, and two sets of red eyes told the detective Frank had broken the news. The couple appeared fit and tanned, and he sensed an aura of wealth, both from their clothes and their bearing. Reggie pegged them in their early fifties.

Frank did the introductions. "Mr. and Mrs. Montrose, this is Detective Brown. He's with Chicago PD's Homicide division."

Neither stood or offered a greeting other than a brief nod, so Reggie took a seat next to Mrs. Montrose. "I'm very sorry for your loss."

The woman managed a weak "thank you," but Mr. Montrose was not interested in the detective's sympathy. "Have you found the animal that did this to our daughter?"

"Sir, as I'm sure Officer Washington explained to you, we first need a positive identification that it *is* your daughter. That has to come before we're allowed to discuss any details relating to the possible homicide."

Mr. Montrose's eyes had dried and his demeanor had suddenly changed. "How and where do we do that?"

Reggie reached into his pocket and extracted one of Janet Thorsen's business cards. "That is the address, and if you would like, you can follow me over there."

"That would be fine. Can we leave now?"

"In just a few minutes. If I can ask you to wait for me in the lobby, I need a few words with Officer Washington before we leave."

Mr. Montrose stood, helping his wife to her feet. "Come on, Darling."

He led her out into the lobby and Reggie shut the door behind them.

Frank sighed. "How do you do it?"

"Do what?"

"Speak to loved ones about their loss. I'm exhausted."

"It comes with the territory, but it never gets any easier."

"I would imagine not."

Reggie sat back down. "Frank, I need you to get back over to the sorority house and make sure my team doesn't need anything."

"Your team?"

"Yeah. I found the spot where I think our perp was hiding, and had forensics come out to process the area."

Frank stood. "I'll get over there now."

Reggie stood with him. "Thanks, but there's something else."

"Okay. Shoot."

"Tammy Williams mentioned a man may have been hanging around some of the sorority houses; are you aware of that?"

"Sure, but I didn't think it was pertinent. The incident took place at a different house from the first victim's, and one of my officers checked it out. After interviewing the guy, he let him go."

"Do you still have the report of that interview?"

"Sure."

"Would you dig it up and fax a copy over to my office?"

"Be glad to. I'll go check on your team first."

"Great. I'll update you after we do the identification."

*Office of
the Medical Examiner
County of Cook
Harrison Street
5:30 p.m.*

The late afternoon traffic slowed their trip across town to the morgue. Despite the hour-long drive, Reggie had not lost the Montroses along the way.

Everyone got out of their vehicles, and Reggie led a nervous procession up the walk and into the building. After speaking with the coroner's assistant on duty, Reggie took Mr. and Mrs. Montrose down a long hallway to a viewing room. Opening the door, he looked at Mr. Montrose. "You'll be able to identify the body in here."

Mr. Montrose turned to his wife and looked into her eyes, shaking his head slowly. "You don't need to see this. Stay out here, okay?"

She nodded without speaking and sat in a chair by the door. Reggie led the man into the chilly room, where they stood in silence, waiting.

A large set of metal double-doors banged open and the tech rolled a sheet-covered gurney into the otherwise empty room. When he'd stopped and locked the wheels in place, he looked up at Reggie. The detective turned to Mr. Montrose. "Whenever you're ready, sir."

The man steeled himself, his resolve apparent on his face, then nodded. The tech lifted the sheet and drew it back from the girl's head. His reaction was immediate and devastating. The sight of his little girl lying before him was too much. Despite his determination, the father's knees buckled, and Reggie had to catch him before he tumbled to the floor.

With the detective's help, Mr. Montrose straightened up, then nodded. "That's our Gina."

Reggie gestured to the tech and he replaced the sheet. Together, the detective and the father moved to the door, and outside to the waiting Mrs. Montrose. When her husband revealed the truth, her reaction mirrored her husband's, and they huddled together while Reggie moved away down the hall. Keeping his back to the couple, he fought to keep his own composure. It seemed the older he got, the harder it became.

****

It took nearly forty-five minutes, but eventually the couple was able to follow the detective back to his desk. Reggie got them each a cup of water before asking them some questions.

"Again, I'm very sorry for your loss."

This time, both nodded their thanks.

"I know this is incredibly difficult, but I must ask."

Mr. Montrose's "take-charge" attitude had returned. "Of course. Anything you need."

"Thank you. When was the last time you spoke with your daughter?"

"Labor Day. She called to say hi to everyone at our family's barbeque. She couldn't make it and just wanted to say she missed us."

"And did she mention any plans of her own?"

"No. I believe she mentioned hanging out with some of her fellow pledges."

"And you hadn't spoken to her since that Monday?"

Montrose shook his head.

Reggie made a note. "Did she mention any trouble with a boyfriend or classmate?"

"Not once."

"What about her former boyfriend? Could he have come to visit her?"

He shook his head. "He's going to school in Texas, and she would have told us if he was coming up."

"Did your daughter seem to be adjusting to college life?"

"As far as we could tell, she was having the time of her life…"

The way he trailed off was Reggie's signal the couple had reached their limit. He put away his notes. "Folks, that's all I need for now. Thank you for coming down."

"Of course. You'll keep us updated on the case, won't you?"

Reggie nodded, handing a card to Mr. Montrose. "You have my word."

CHICAGO HOMICIDE

<u>Saturday, September 6</u>

Homicide Squad Room
Area 5 Precinct
9:30 a.m.

Reggie arrived later than normal to find the lieutenant's office empty, but his own desk full. The forensic report, the autopsy findings, and the incident file from Frank were all waiting for him. He filled his coffee mug and gathered all three reports into a pile. Taking advantage of the quiet in the lieutenant's office, he shut the door and started in on the stack of reading.

The forensic report was on top and seemed as good a place as any to start.

Victim's cell phone—only prints belong to the victim. No blood or other biological material detected.

Cigarette butt—sent to lab for DNA analysis—results pending.

Plaster cast of Footprint— approximately thirty percent of sole pattern

*is distinct—men's athletic shoe—size range
8 1/2 to 10—brand undetermined.*

He closed the file. All in all, he had
nothing to go on, unless of course the killer
shared the cigarette with his victim. The
wide range of shoe size from the plaster
print was even less help.

Getting up and going to his desk, he
found a chart he kept under his calendar and
ran his finger down the first column. Using
the shoe size, it gave a height estimate for
the wearer, which narrowed his suspect list
to men between five-foot-eight and six foot.

*My suspect pool is now down to about
half a million!*

He went back to the lieutenant's desk
and opened the autopsy findings. It served as
a mirror image of the Addison scene. Cause
of death: strangulation, likely by the same
double-wire garrote, and there was no sign
of rape. Gina had been dead less than twelve
hours at time of her discovery, and no trace
evidence had been recovered from the body.

Strike two!

Last on the pile was the report from
Central College security about the man seen
hanging around the sorority houses. Reggie
scanned the top page.

The responding officer was Bill
Brunner, who encountered the man behind

the Alpha Chi Omega house. The individual gave his name as Nate Tucker, which the officer verified by checking the man's license. Nathaniel Tucker, age twenty-seven, was asked why he was wandering around the sorority house, to which he responded that his girlfriend had dumped him and he was looking for her to "fix" things. Tucker had refused to give the girlfriend's name.

When he was searched, a knife was found in his possession and confiscated. No prosecutable violation had occurred, so the officer escorted Tucker off the college campus, and instructed him not to return.

Reggie returned to his own desk and fired up his computer. Doing a record search for the name Nathaniel Tucker, he got an immediate hit.

Nathaniel J. Tucker had been arrested on several occasions, dating back to his late teens. His first brushes with authorities were petty in nature, but by the time he was twenty-one, he'd graduated to major crimes, including a rape. He did five years in Joliet before being released thirteen months ago, and his one-year probation just ended.

Reggie checked the photo. Black, five-nine, and a hundred-forty-five pounds; he fit the witness account and shoe imprint.

So do the other half-million possibles!

Still, one thing was different; Tucker could be placed on the school campus at least once.

Reggie dialed Frank.

"Security." The voice was female.

"Is Frank Washington there?"

"Not at the moment. Can I give him a message?"

Reggie played a hunch. "Is Bill Brunner there?"

"Hold, please."

Thirty seconds later, a male voice came on. "This is Officer Brunner."

"Yes, this is Detective Brown with Chicago PD."

"Hey, Detective. Frank's out at the moment."

"Actually, I wanted to speak to you."

"Oh? Okay, shoot."

"Do you recall an encounter with a Nate Tucker?"

"Sure; last week. Why?"

"In your report, you mentioned confiscating a knife from him. Do you still have it?"

"It was Frank who took possession of the knife so I'll have to check the evidence locker to see if it's still there."

Reggie picked up the report from his desk. "Did you say Frank took possession of the knife?"

"Yeah. Why?"

"I didn't see his name listed as a responding officer on the paperwork you filed."

"No, you wouldn't. He told me to leave it off because he wasn't actually on duty; hc just happened to be around the campus at the time."

"I see." Reggie wasn't sure he did but let it go. "Can you check on the knife for me?"

"Sure. Hold on."

Reggie waited, only able to hear some shuffling in the background. It was probably five minutes or more before Brunner came back on the line. "It's still here."

"Do you return confiscated items?"

"The owner can come by and request it. Most of the time, they don't."

Reggie's pulse ticked up a notch. "Can you hold it for me? I'd like to have it tested."

"I don't see any problem with it. I'll make Frank aware and you can clear it with him when you come after it."

"Will he be there today?"

"Should be back anytime."

"Great; thanks."

Reggie hung up, grateful to have at least one lead to follow up on. It was nearly noon and his stomach was complaining of being empty. He headed for *B & B*.

Security Offices
Central College of Chicago
Norwood Park
1:30 p.m.

Frank was talking to a student in the security office lobby when Reggie arrived. Frank held up a finger when he saw Reggie, so the detective grabbed a seat in Frank's office. Laying on the desk, wrapped in an evidence bag, was a knife.

Frank came in moments later. "Hi, Reggie."

"Hey, Frank. Is that the knife?"

"That's it." The security chief grabbed the bag and tossed it to Reggie. "Brunner told me you'd be after it."

Reggie studied it briefly, then tucked it away. Frank had dropped into his chair and was watching the detective, who met his gaze. "You didn't mention you were there when Nathaniel Tucker was questioned."

A brief moment of silence overtook the room, until Frank's face broke into a wide grin. "Yeah, I know. I got Tucker confused with another case, and thought I was at the other one. I do that on a regular basis."

"What's that? Get confused?"

Frank gave a half-hearted laugh. "That, too. Actually, I often come around campus in the evenings minus my uniform. I like to see what's going on when students don't know security is around."

Reggie smiled. "Oh. Seems like a good idea."

"I think so."

Reggie switched gears. "I've got something you could help me with."

"Fire away."

"Is there an office or person who oversees sororities on campus?"

"There is; OSFL."

"OSFL?"

Frank waved a hand in the manner of apology. "Sorry. The Office of Sorority-Fraternity Life. They're the administration's oversight group of Greek life at the college."

"Is there someone over there I could speak with? I'd like to ask a few questions about the sororities our victims came from."

"Sure. Let me give Annette a call."

****

Within just a couple minutes, Frank had arranged a meeting and they were headed across campus. Located on the ground floor of a co-ed residence hall, OSFL was a brightly lit and modern office space in stark contrast to the colonial design of the hall itself.

A young lady smiled as they approached, her brunette ponytail swaying back and forth as she talked. "Hi, Mr. Washington. Miss Roderick is expecting you."

"Thank you."

Reggie followed Frank through a large wood door into an expansive area. Surprisingly, the colonial style returned in the dark paneling and high, arching windows. Annette Roderick moved out from behind a car-sized desk with her hand extended.

"Frank, good to see you."

They shook hands, then Frank turned to Reggie. "Annette, this is Detective Brown with Chicago Homicide."

Reggie shook her hand, impressed by her firm grip. Tall with blonde hair and high cheekbones, her European heritage was obvious. "Pleased to meet you, Detective."

"Please, call me Reggie. Thank you for making time to see me."

"Of course. I can't begin to describe the impact these events have had on our campus and students. Is there any progress in finding out who did this?"

"We're evaluating several leads at this time."

"Good." She pointed to some upholstered chairs in front of her desk. "Please sit."

Reggie accepted the offer and pulled out his notepad. Annette moved back behind her desk and dropped into a plush high-back chair. "Now, how can I help?"

"The two sororities involved—Gamma Sigma Delta and Kappa Gamma Phi—do they stand out in any way?"

"How do you mean?"

"Well, for instance, have there been any issues with violence before?"

"Not that I'm aware of."

"How about the adding of new members? Has either sorority had any issues with their pledges before?"

Confusion mixed with concern revealed itself on her face. "I'm not sure what you're driving at, Detective."

"Hazing. Is it an issue with these two sororities?"

Miss Roderick appeared as if he'd just thrown a hand grenade in her lap. Startled, she crossed her arms and leaned back in her chair. "Detective…"

"Reggie is fine."

"Very well, Reggie. Hazing, in *any* form, is not tolerated on this campus. We've not had a single case documented in the eight years I've been here."

Reggie had done his homework. "I understand that, ma'am, and it's not my intention to offend anyone. However, there have been at least three reports made to Chicago PD of suspected violations of that policy."

"*Suspected* violations, Detective."

"Yes, ma'am. I know there were never charges filed, but I'm looking for any suggestion of violence that may separate either of these two sororities from others on campus."

She stared at him hard, seeming to be re-gathering herself. "The answer to your question is no; neither sorority has issues similar to what you describe. As you have probably already discovered, neither sorority was involved in the three instances you referred to, either."

"Yes, ma'am. What about the pledge class as a whole? How many do you have this year?"

"Our pledge class spread between eight sororities is around seven hundred fifty young women."

"And about how many will receive an offer to join?"

"It's hard to say. Roughly half, maybe less."

"So, there's competition for the slots?"

"Yes, but it doesn't lead to violence on the level you're suggesting."

"What level would you say the violence does reach?"

Anger surged across the women's face. "Don't twist my words, Detective."

"I'm sorry, it wasn't my intention. One more question."

"Of course."

"Do any of the fraternities have issues with their sister clubs?"

"No."

The emphatic tone of her answer spoke volumes. He folded his notepad up. "Very good. Thank you for your time, Miss Roderick."

Frank, who hadn't said a word, got up. "Thanks, Annette. We'll get out of your hair now."

"Any time, Frank."

Reggie didn't get the same invitation.

Homicide Squad Room
Area 5 Precinct
4:45 p.m.

After dropping off the knife for forensic testing, Reggie finally got back to his desk. Waiting for him were the phone records from both throwaway phones, one used to warn Chad about the next victim, and the other about the body of Gina Montrose.

Each record consisted of a single sheet of paper containing a single call, which bounced off of the same cell tower. Reggie checked the tower number: Navy Pier. If Grant Park was a tough place to find someone, Navy Pier was impossible.

Also located on the Chicago lakefront, the Navy Pier was one of the most visited destinations for tourists in the entire Midwest. Thirty-four acres of museums, shops, restaurants, and stores, and even if it were possible to track down exactly where the call came from, he'd never be able to learn who made it.

Reggie stared at the report for a few minutes longer, and though he couldn't put his finger on it, he was missing something. He rubbed his eyes, weariness washing over him.

Come on, Reg. Get this old brain of yours working.

Finally, he gave up and called Sonya.

"Hello?"

"Hey, Honey. Did you get hold of the doctor?"

"A specialist on a Saturday? Reggie, I'm good, but I'm not that good!"

He laughed. "I'm getting ready to leave."

"Okay. Both dinner and I will be waiting for you."

He smiled—something she could always get him to do when he was down—and let go with a low whistle into the phone. "You sure know how to spoil me."

"See you soon."

He hung up, suddenly not as weary, and headed for the car.

CHICAGO HOMICIDE

Sunday, September 7

*Home of
Sonya & Reggie Brown
Eastside Neighborhood
1:10 p.m.*

They arrived home from church just in time to get the call from their daughter, Nina. She'd taken a teaching position in Tampa, Florida, after college and a Sunday phone call had become their ritual. Sonya was first through the door and reached the phone.

"Hello?"

"Hi, Momma."

"Hi, Nina. We just got in from church."

"How was it?"

"Nice; Pastor said a prayer for your father."

Nina laughed. "Daddy needs all the prayers he can get!"

"You're right about that."

"No result from the biopsy?"

"Not yet, and it could be Tuesday or Wednesday before we hear. How are things at work?"

"Good. My new group of kids is a handful, but I love them. Can I talk to Daddy?"

"Of course; love you."

Sonya handed the phone to Reggie.

"Hi, Daddy."

"Hi, Baby. It's good to hear your voice."

"Yours too. How are you feeling?"

Reggie smirked at his wife. "I'm fine, Nina. You and your mother are worry-warts."

She scoffed at her father's bluster. "You know as well as we do, this is serious."

"Yes, of course. I just don't like seeing the two most important women in my life upset."

"It's only because we love you."

"I love you, too. How's the new class?"

"Exciting. What about you? Are looking forward to the big day?"

"I guess. I'm excited to have more time with your mother, but…"

"But what?"

"Oh, I'm working a case and would hate to leave it unsolved." Sonya was watching him, and had fixed him with a knowing grin. "Anyway, we'll see. Maybe I'll have it all wrapped up by then."

"Is Mom giving you the evil eye?"

"Oh yeah!"

Nina laughed. "I'll let you go then."

"Love you, Nina. Bye."

Reggie hung up the phone as Sonya disappeared into the kitchen. Reggie went and changed out of his church clothes, returning a few minutes later in sweats and a t-shirt, his usual Sunday afternoon attire. Sonya was on the couch and on the table in front of her were two sandwiches and two glasses of milk.

He sat next to her and sipped his milk. "Thanks."

"You're welcome."

They ate in silence, and when Sonya stood to take the plates to the kitchen, Reggie reached up and pulled her back down next to him. She refused to meet his gaze.

"Sonya, what is it?"

"It's nothing."

It's most certainly something.

He touched her chin and turned her face toward him. Reflected in her brown eyes was not anger, but pain. "Come on, out with it."

Tears welled up as she met his gaze. "I feel like you don't want to retire and spend time with me."

His eyes widened in surprise. "Why would you think that?"

She shrugged. "I don't know. It seems like every time we discuss your last day, you act like I'm dragging you into the next part of our life together?"

It was Reggie's turn to feel pain. His heart broke as the realization of what she was saying hit him. "Awww baby, nothing could be further from the truth. I can't wait for you and me to move on."

She smiled despite the tears running down her cheeks. "It doesn't feel that way."

"I can see that now, and I'm sorry."

"You've given thirty years to the force; isn't that long enough?"

"Without a doubt, but it's not about that."

"What then?"

He took both her hands and stared into her eyes. "If, and only if, I extend my time at work, it will be for just a few days. Young women are dying, and I'm afraid the time it would take to bring another detective up to speed on the case might result in another girl dying unnecessarily. If I'm close to solving it, I'd want to see it out. But, if it's going cold, or looking like we'll need a lucky break, I will turn it over."

She leaned in against his chest. "Promise?"

"You have my word."

"Well okay, but if you go past the fifteenth, it's gonna cost you dearly."

He laughed and squeezed her tight. "I have no doubt!"

CHICAGO HOMICIDE

<u>Monday, September 8</u>

Production Meeting Room
WWND-10 Studios
North Center
7:45 a.m.

Vince closed the door and leaned against it. Chad, standing just inside, played the message.

"The police aren't telling you everything. The dead girls' pledge pins are in their mouths."

Vince shook his head. "That's sick."
"I guess I should call Brown."
"To do what? Verify?"
"No. I'm supposed to tell him when there's a new message."
"Are you crazy? This is a goldmine."
"Vince, I'm not sure withholding this is a good idea. Can't we get in trouble?"
Vince shook his head. "Lives aren't at risk this time and it's not a threat. It's just information."
Chad appeared conflicted. "I guess."

Vince pointed at a chair. "Sit down, Chad. There are things happening behind the scenes that you're not aware of."

"Like what?"

Vince moved to the door. "Just sit tight for a minute and don't do anything."

The work and stress of the last few days was beginning to catch up with the reporter. He sighed. "Fine."

Vince left the room, returning moments later with Shawna Reilly. Barely over five feet tall, with shoulder-length red hair and penetrating green eyes, she came into the room like a fireball. Vince hadn't yet closed the door before she was sitting across from Chad. "Let me hear it."

Chad did.

Reilly listened with her eyes closed. "Play it again, please."

A second time, Chad ran the message. When it finished, Reilly opened her eyes and rotated to look at her associate producer. "This is perfect."

Vince nodded. "That's what I thought. If I could have ordered up something, it wouldn't have been this good."

Chad was becoming exasperated. "Ordered up for what? Would someone please tell me what's going on?"

Reilly turned back to her reporter. "Chad, the news gods have smiled down on you again."

"How so?"

"Your reports have been followed by corporate in New York. They've been in touch with me about taking the story national."

Chad stared at her, mouth hanging open. It was so fast and the story still so young. His mind traveled to the national exposure he'd receive, the very thing every local reporter was after. Getting noticed was half the battle when it came to moving up in the news business, especially if you didn't have connections, which Chad certainly didn't. "Are you serious?"

Reilly nodded. "They were waiting for something to make it more of a national interest than just Chicago or the Midwest, and that message is it. They'll eat it up, I'm sure."

Reilly turned back to Vince, her famous energy already pushing forward at full steam. "I'll need to verify with New York, then we can decide on a location, set-up, and script. New York will want to see a rough draft before we go live."

Vince was making notes. He was as pumped as Reilly. "I'm all over it. How long before we get confirmation from corporate?"

"I'll put in the call now and let you know as soon as I have something." Reilly stood and moved to the door.

Vince looked over at Chad. "We'll start bouncing ideas around on how to use the message."

"Yeah, but shouldn't I call Detective Brown."

Reilly stopped and spun to look at the young reporter. "Absolutely not!"

Chad had heard stories of Reilly's eyes narrowing like a cat's, but didn't believe them until now. "I could get in trouble though, can't I?"

Reilly took a couple steps toward him. "Look Chad, this is it for you. Stories don't get much bigger for a reporter at the affiliate level. Do you understand that?"

He nodded, his eyes locked with hers.

"So, you have a choice. You can report this to the detective—and risk the story being leaked by someone else—or wait until after the report to make the call. But know this, if you call and we're scooped, your chances of ever moving up will be gone."

The force of their stares bore down on him as he weighed his decision.

The message is not a warning or a threat.

It's not going to lead to the guy's capture.

Besides, I'm entitled to use a source without permission from the police, aren't I?

He looked up at Reilly. "The message gave me an idea for naming the story: The Pledge Pin Killer."

A smile worked its way across Reilly's face. "I like it."

She returned to the door and opened it. "Get to work gentlemen—and don't forget—New York is an hour ahead of us."

Homicide Squad Room
Area 5 Precinct
8:30 a.m.

Reggie arrived at the precinct to find two messages on his desk. The first was from the forensics lab.

The knife left for testing on 9/6 was wiped clean of prints. DNA found within the lock-back device was sent for testing.

Reggie stared at the note. It didn't make any sense that the knife wouldn't have prints.

The note said it had been wiped, but why? And by who?

He was pondering those questions when the second note caught his eye. Despite his request that the doctor's office inform Sonya about the biopsy result, they had called his work instead. His pulse accelerated as he dialed the number.

"Good morning; Dr. Scott's office."

"Yes, this is Reggie Brown. I had a message to call."

"Yes, Mr. Brown; please hold."

Reggie's blood pressure slowly climbed as he waited.

"Reggie?"

"Yes?"

"This is Jim Scott."

"Hi, Doc. Apparently, you have my results?"

"I do indeed. So, it's one of those bad news—good news deals. The bad news is the biopsy came back positive for cancer; the good news is that it's not melanoma."

Reggie lowered himself into his chair. "Okay…"

"Well, essentially, you have skin cancer that needs to be surgically removed.

The important factor here is the type: basal cell carcinoma."

Reggie had heard the name from Sonya but couldn't remember the significance. "That's important why?"

"Two reasons. First, it's very slow growing, and second, it's unlikely to have metastasized."

Reggie's head was spinning. "Metastasized?"

"Spread."

"I see. So, what do we do next?"

"My physician assistant is going to get in touch with a friend of mine who specializes in these surgeries. You should get a call with a schedule in the next few days."

"Okay. Thanks, Doc."

"My pleasure. Try not to worry too much; I think your prognosis is very good. Take care."

The line went dead and Reggie hung up.

I have skin cancer.

The words echoed in his brain.

Suddenly, the life he and Sonya had talked about for so long wasn't a given. Yet, the doctor hadn't sounded overly concerned.

Sure! It's not his cancer.

himself together and
ant's office. Jerry Davis
ggie. Need something?"
to run home for a few
rest of the day."
rerything alright?"
ll talk to you later."

Home of
Sonya & Reggie Brown
Eastside Neighborhood
9:30 a.m.

Sonya was just finishing up some laundry when she heard the front door open. "Reggie, is that you?"

"Yeah."

She came around the corner to find him standing at the fridge, pouring himself some juice. "What are you doing home?"

He returned the pitcher to the fridge and took a long drink. "I heard from the doctor."

Sonya's breath froze in her chest. "And?"

He pulled out a chair at the kitchen table and sat down, pushing the chair across from him out with his foot. "Sit with me."

She did. "You're scaring me, Reggie."

Finally, he smiled slightly. "I'm sorry, I'm not meaning to. Dr. Scott called with the result. He said the biopsy came back as positive for cancer."

Her eyes instantly filled with tears, but she fought to remain calm. The answer to her next question meant everything. "What kind?"

"Basal cell carcinoma."

She finally took a breath. "Not melanoma?"

He shook his head.

"Did Dr. Scott say anything else?"

"Yes. Most importantly, he thought my prognosis was very good, but it will require surgery."

"What if it has spread?"

"That would not be a good thing, but he felt it was unlikely."

Sonya had done some research, and with what she'd learned, there was no doubt the result could have been worse. Still, like many of her friends, cancer's dark shadow had pushed itself into their lives. The results could be devastating, but she decided right then and there, that wouldn't be the case for her Reggie.

She took his hand and squeezed it. "Do you have to go back to the station?"

He shrugged. "I don't have anything pressing for once."

"Good. I'll get dressed and we'll go somewhere."

"That sounds nice; I'll let Jerry know."

She smiled, kissed his forehead, and went to change.

****

Sonya was their guide for the afternoon, taking them first to Millennium Park. The day was clear and warm as they walked the Chase Promenade, holding hands, their focus on each other. Grinning like tourists, they posed for a selfie in front of the Cloud Gate, a giant reflective sculpture in the shape of a kidney bean.

As early afternoon came, they crossed the Michigan Avenue Bridge, stopping to look east along the Chicago River, before moving up the Magnificent Mile. Passing the Wrigley Building and the Tribune Tower, she surprised Reggie when she stopped and turned into Michael Jordan's Steak House.

It had been several years since they'd eaten there, so they lingered over wine in the subdued atmosphere. By the time they arrived home in the early evening, Sonya felt better than she had in years. Her Reggie was going to be fine, and *they* were going to be fine.

She poured them each a cup of coffee and they settled in to watch the evening news.

Broadcast Control Room
WWND-10 Studios
North Center
5:00 p.m.

Shawna Reilly closed the door, lit up the red "On Air" sign, and moved to her customary place behind the technical director.

In front of them was a bank of ten clearly labeled monitors. Directly in front was *On Air*, surrounded by three different *studio cams*, three *remote location* monitors,

149

two *video tape* screens, and a *live network* feed.

Shawna checked the status of each.

On Air was showing a Simpsons repeat. The studio cams were focused on the empty anchor desk. The live network feed ran the ongoing national news from New York.

Camera one of the remote screens showed Chad Marshall standing in front of the brick arch that served as the main entrance to the Central College campus. He was checking notes and fixing his hair, fidgeting more than Shawna was used to seeing. She couldn't blame him; it was his first national report.

Shawna picked up the phone. "Vince, you there?"

"Yeah, Shawna."

"Is Chad ready to go?"

"Yes."

"Okay, six minutes. New York will come out of commercial and send it— Chad sends it back. Myles Hardy is the anchor on the national broadcast tonight."

"Got it."

The other phone line in the room lit up. "This is Reilly."

"Shawna, this is Jack in New York. Is your guy standing by?"

"All set."

"Okay. Patch our audio through to him and be ready. Four minutes."

Shawna tapped her technical director on the shoulder and the national audio went out to Chad. His face told her he had received it.

Shawna keyed the mic in front of her, letting her into Chad's ear as well. "Okay Chad, three minutes."

He nodded at the camera.

Shawna watched the clock. "Two minutes; they're in commercial."

Scanning the shot, she checked for the hundredth time to make sure she hadn't missed something. It looked solid.

"One minute."

Seconds later, the smooth baritone of Myles Hardy filled her senses.

"Tonight, we check in with the events surrounding two murders in Chicago. Recent evidence suggests that a serial killer is at large, and the case has taken a bizarre turn. Reporting for us from our affiliate WWND in Chicago is Chad Marshall."

"Good Evening, Myles. I'm standing in front of the gates to Central College of Chicago, home to two students who have died at the hands of 'The Pledge Pin Killer'."

The camera moved to the school's name before a pair of high school graduation photos, each girl in their cap and gown, appeared on the screen.

"Both women, Mackenzie Addison and Gina Montrose, were attending Central College when they went missing. Their bodies were later found in two separate wooded areas of the city, partially nude, and most disturbingly, with their sorority pledge pins lodged inside their throats. It is that detail, along with other evidence, that has revealed the connection between the two murders. While they had pledged to different sororities, both girls had just started their lives as college freshman, only to have them cut short by a madman."

The camera returned to Chad.

"At this time, no suspect has been officially identified by Chicago police. As you can imagine, the city of Chicago, and the large university community in particular, remain on edge."

"Reporting for ABC News, I'm Chad Marshall in Chicago."

"Thank you, Chad. In other news…"

Shawna tapped her technical director's shoulder, who shut down the audio patch to New York. She pumped her fist in the air. "That was awesome!"

Grabbing Vince's line, she yelled into the phone. "Nice job, Vince!"

"Everything look good there, Shawna?"

"Perfect. Hold on, the other line is ringing." She switched calls. "Reilly."

"Shawna, Jack here. Tell your boy nice work, and keep us up to date on developments."

"You got it, Jack."

The line went dead and she transferred back over to Vince. "New York loved it, Vince. Tell Chad they said so."

"I will. Are we leading with another live report on local at six?"

"Yes."

"Okay, we'll be ready."

Home of
Sonya & Reggie Brown
Eastside Neighborhood
5:20 p.m.

While sitting together on the couch, enjoying coffee and reflecting on their day together, Sonya sensed her husband's body stiffen. She looked up at the TV to see what had grabbed his attention. Reggie pushed the volume up on the remote.

"At this time, no suspect has been officially identified by Chicago police. As you can imagine, the city of Chicago, and the large university community in particular, remain on edge. Reporting for ABC News, I'm Chad Marshall in Chicago."

Reggie stood and began pacing. "Son of a… What is he trying to do? The idiot is gonna start a panic!"

Sonya watched her husband move back and forth across the living room floor. "What is it, Reggie?"

"Did you hear what he said?"

"Chad Marshall?"

"Yeah. The Pledge Pin Killer! He's not even supposed to know about the pins."

"What are you talking about? What pins?"

He stopped pacing and took a deep breath. "I'm sorry; I know you're in the dark about this. The killer leaves the girl's sorority pledge pins inside their mouths as a signature."

Reggie didn't share the gruesome details of his job with her very often, and with good reason. She preferred not to know what he had to deal with. "That's awful!"

He had regained his composure. "I know, and I'm sorry I dumped that on you."

The phone rang and Reggie snatched it up. "Hello?"

"Reggie, this is Jerry. What in the name of all that's holy just happened?"

"I gather you saw the news."

"Actually, no. But, the chief saw it and he is hot! Did you know Marshall was going on air with that information?"

"I did not."

"Well, how did he get it?"

"I don't know, Jerry. I can only suppose he got another message from the killer."

His boss sighed. "Alright, here's the deal. Find out what happened and be ready for a news conference tomorrow afternoon.

155

It's you and me with the chief, and we better have answers."

"I'm on it."

"You better be! I don't want your last case to turn into a nightmare, Reg."

"Me either, Jerry."

Reggie hung up. *It's too late for that now.*

He dialed Chad's number. After two rings, it went to voicemail.

"This is Brown. I need you to be at the station in the morning, eight sharp! And don't make me come looking for you, Marshall."

He slammed the phone down. Sonya sat quietly, sad the evening news had buried all the tranquility from their peaceful afternoon. She focused on the many more days they would have like the afternoon they just enjoyed to fight back tears.

Tuesday, September 9

Homicide Squad Room
Area 5 Precinct
7:45 a.m.

Reggie arrived at his desk to find a DNA report waiting for him. A scowl worked its way across his face as he read it.

DNA profile from subject knife submitted on 9/6 is unidentified and does not match DNA profile from victim one's nail trimmings.

Nate Tucker was not his man.

He grabbed his cup and got some fresh coffee. When he returned to his desk, Chad was standing there. "Good morning, Detective."

For a moment, Reggie just stared at him. Finally, he turned and headed for an interview room. "Follow me."

Once inside, they sat across from each other at a small table, and Reggie took out his notepad. The reporter was having trouble meeting the detective's stare. "Would you like to tell me where you got the information for your report last night?"

"About the pins?"

"Yes, about the pins! Don't play dumb with me, Marshall."

"I received another message from the killer."

"The Pledge Pin Killer, you mean." Sarcasm oozed from every pore of the big detective's body.

"Uh… yeah."

"Let me hear it."

Chad pulled out his phone and played the message for Reggie. After making some notes, the detective looked up at Chad, who was still doing his best to avoid eye contact. "Why didn't you let me know first?"

"My A.P. and news director wanted to run the story before I called you. They were afraid we'd get scooped."

"You mean, the story would be leaked, is that it?"

Chad nodded.

Reggie sighed. "What makes you think I would leak any part of an ongoing investigation?"

Chad shrugged.

"Who or what is your A.P?"

"Vince Henderson; he's my producer. Ever since this began, he's been trying to get me to withhold the info until after we go on the air."

Reggie jotted down the producer's name. "What is your news director's name?"

"Shawna Reilly."

Reggie noted it too. "So, what was different about this information that you obliged?"

"It wasn't a threat or a warning."

Reggie leaned back and stared at the reporter, weighing his options. "This Vince Henderson, why is he so willing to obstruct justice?"

The impact of the phrase "obstruct justice" was immediate and served its purpose. Chad started backpedaling immediately. "Hey, come on, Reggie. Nobody is talking about obstruction of justice here."

"Really? I have to meet with my chief today, and my guess is he'll be talking about just that, as well as tampering with evidence in an ongoing murder investigation."

"Nobody is trying to break the law; we used our best judgement on a news story. It's something we do every day."

Reggie sat forward, getting very close to the reporter, who slid slightly backward in his seat. "Let me tell you what that judgement has resulted in: Near panic among the women of CCC; an exodus of female students from college campuses across the city; and a major compromise of a critical detail that could have identified the killer."

Chad's shoulders sagged as he stared at the floor. He did not intend to attempt to defend his decision.

Reggie wasn't done. "What is Henderson's stake in trying to convince you to withhold the recordings?"

"Simple; headlines. He said himself: *If I could have ordered up something, it wouldn't have been that good.*"

"I see." Reggie put away his pad. "Here's how this is going to play out. I'm gonna do everything I can to keep you and your crew from being charged, but in return, I expect this to never happen again. Is that clear?"

Chad nodded.

"I don't care who wants you to hold off, if it happens again, I'll drop a pile of charges on you guys that's so deep, you'll have no time to report anything for a month! Are we understanding each other?"

"Loud and clear."

"Good. Now, get out of here."

*Office of
Lieutenant Jerry Davis
Area 5 Precinct
10:15 a.m.*

"Reggie!" He turned around to see Jerry Davis standing at his office door. "Got a minute?"

Without waiting for an answer, his boss went back into his office.

Reggie pulled himself up and followed. "Good morning, Jerry."

"Maybe; that depends on what you have to tell me."

Reggie dropped into a chair across from his lieutenant. "I met with Marshall first thing this morning. He claimed his superiors pressured him into keeping the latest call until after the news report."

"A call from the killer revealing a critical detail of the crimes. Did it occur to him to check the validity of that detail with us?"

Reggie shrugged. "If it did, he didn't say so."

Jerry rubbed his eyes with both hands, already tired despite the early hour. "Chief Madison was fit to be tied. The mayor called him and reamed him for allowing a panic to start in the city. He made sure Madison understood how critical the college community was to the financial well-being of this city, and therefore, the police chief's job."

"I'm sorry, Jerry. I was blindsided like everyone else."

Jerry leaned back in his chair. "I know you were. Have we impressed upon Mr. Marshall how important his cooperation is from now on?"

"I think he got the message loud and clear."

"What about his superiors?"

"Actually, the producer in charge of Chad's stories seems to be the main problem. I thought I would rattle his cage later today."

"Good. Now, tell me where we're at with the case."

Reggie held his hands out with the palms up. "I've got nothing, or almost nothing. There's the DNA from under the first victim's fingernails, but so far no matches. The phones were throwaways used in extremely busy locations and have yielded very little. In fact, here's the number from the latest call; I need the records."

"I'll handle it right away. What about the killer himself? Any insight into who we might be looking for?"

"Just general stuff. He seems to be comfortable on the college campus; the second victim was snatched from behind a dorm building. Also, he appears to be familiar with the city; both dump sites were the kind of place locals are more apt to know."

"What about motive?"

"Again, not much. The girls weren't raped but their underwear was missing, giving it a sexual overtone, but the sorority pins indicate something different."

"Such as?"

"That's the thing, I'm not sure. Anger at sorority girls, a grudge against particular sororities, or some kind of beef with CCC."

"What about the girls themselves? Was there anything to indicate they were specifically targeted?"

Reggie shrugged again. "Not that I can find. They didn't know each other, they traveled in different circles, and there was no obvious enemy I could find in either one's life."

Jerry stared at the ceiling and rubbed his neck for a long time. Finally, he sat forward. "Okay, the press conference with Chief Madison is scheduled for one. Our line will be that the public should stay vigilant and cautious, but that there's no need to panic; nothing indicates that the average citizen has anything to fear."

"Can we say that comfortably?"

"It doesn't matter if *we're* comfortable, Reggie. It matters if the *public* is."

Reggie had been doing this long enough to understand how it worked, and more importantly, that these decisions weren't up to him. He looked at his watch. "I'm gonna grab some lunch before the big show. You want something?"

"Where are you going?"

"Burger King."

"Yeah, grab me a whopper and fries?"

"You bet."

City Hall Press Room Downtown Chicago 1:00 p.m.

The seat of Cook County, and the home of Chicago's power brokers, took up an entire block downtown. The eleven-story, stone structure featured marble stairs, cavernous halls and a rooftop garden with a honey bee colony that produced over two-hundred pounds of honey a year.

The teak-paneled pressroom was not large by any standard. So it was overflowing with press representatives when Reggie, Jerry, and Chief Madison walked out to the oak podium at the front of the room. Chief Madison moved to the microphone while Reggie and Jerry stood behind him, their eyes focused on the back wall, hands clasped in front of them.

Madison tapped the mic, heard a thump, and began.

"Thank you for coming today. As you are aware, just since Labor Day, two young women from one of our college campuses have lost their lives. Our hearts and prayers go out to their families, and we wish to assure them we are doing everything we can to both find, and stop, the one who visited this tragedy upon them."

Reggie locked eyes with Chad, who was leaning against a doorframe along the side of the room, his producer and cameraman next to him. They were one of nearly half a dozen TV crews.

Madison continued. "The purpose of this news conference is to reassure the public that there is no immediate danger to the citizens of our great city. While no arrest has been made, the case is our top priority, and no effort is being spared in our attempt to find the killer. Having said that, it is critical that all Chicagoans, both on and off our city's college campuses, be vigilant and wary of their surroundings. If you see anything suspicious, please call 9-1-1."

The chief turned and looked at the men standing behind him. "I'm going to turn the microphone over to Lieutenant Davis and Detective Brown, and they will take your questions."

Mayor Madison stepped back as Jerry and Reggie moved forward. Several hands went up and Jerry pointed.

"Lieutenant Davis, is there a person or persons of interest at this time?"

"There are several people we are doing background on, but no official suspects have been named."

A woman stood in the front row. "What kind of evidence do you have, besides the pins?"

"The gathering of evidence is an ongoing process. At this time, we are looking at both electronic and forensic evidence."

A man stood. "Is it fair to say the Pledge Pin Killer will strike again?"

Davis shook his head. "We have no way of knowing that. As the chief said, we want everyone to be cautious regardless."

The lieutenant nodded toward a long-time Chicago Tribune reporter. "Yes?"

"My question is for Detective Brown."

Reggie leaned closer to the mic and his own voice surprised him. "Go... Go ahead."

"Detective, if I'm not mistaken, you have a daughter who recently graduated college."

Reggie's pulse surged. "Yes."

"If she was here today, would you tell her it's okay to go to classes at CCC or any other university in the Chicago area?"

All eyes were fixed on Reggie, including the mayor's. The only sound in the room was the air blowing from the overhead vents. "Well, the point is moot since my daughter doesn't do what I tell her anyway."

Laughter filled the room, and Reggie felt Jerry nudge him aside. When everyone had settled down, Jerry finished answering the question.

"Look, whether there's currently someone seeking to hurt our sons and daughters or not, our young people need to be aware of their surroundings, and look out for each other. Thank you for your time."

Just like that, the conference was over, and the chief's press secretary steered all three officers out of the room. Back in the mayor's office, Chief Madison smiled at Reggie. "Well done, Detective. That was fast thinking."

"Thank you, sir."

Reggie and Jerry headed back to the precinct, both relieved to have the conference over with and be able to get back to work. As they got in the car, Jerry grinned at his friend. "How did you think of that so fast, Reg?"

"Simple; I told the truth."

WWND-10 Studios
North Center
3:45 p.m.

Reggie stopped at the front desk and waited for the receptionist to finish on the phone. When she hung up, she turned her bright smile toward the detective. "Can I help you?"

Reggie showed his badge and her smile disappeared. "My name is Detective Brown. I'd like to speak with Vince Henderson, please."

"Let me check if he's in."

While she placed a call to Henderson, Reggie studied the awards on the wall behind the desk. Multiple plaques denoting achievement for reporting, programming, and community service hung haphazardly across the space. Also, there were photos of the station employees, and Reggie took particular interest in studying the faces of Vince Henderson and Shawna Reilly.

"Detective?"

"Yes?"

"If you'll go down that hallway to the right, Mr. Henderson will meet you at the end."

"Thank you."

As Reggie made his way down the long passage framed by glass walls on either side, he could see the inner workings of the newsroom. Multiple TV monitors hanging from the ceiling around a large, carpeted room, carried different news and sports stations. Most had headlines scrolling across the bottom.

Cubicle groupings of six or eight stations were randomly positioned around the space, all sporting blinking computer monitors, with about half the stations occupied by someone typing or talking on the phone.

At the end of the hall, Vince Henderson stepped out and waved at Reggie. When the detective reached him, Vince extended his hand. "Detective Brown, I'm Vince Henderson. Nice to meet you."

"Thank you for seeing me."

"Of course." They shook hands, and Vince escorted the detective into a large meeting room. Also equipped with TV monitors hanging at one end, the room was dominated by a long wood table. Vince gestured toward a chair, then sat across from Reggie. "Would you like something to drink?"

"No, thank you." Reggie took out his notepad. "I just have a few questions."

"By all means."

"You serve as producer for all of Chad Marshall's stories, is that right?"

"Yes."

"And he runs his story ideas by you, then you run them past News Director Reilly, correct?"

"Correct."

"It's my understanding that you and the news director have been hindering my investigation."

"I'm sorry?"

"I am told you've been putting pressure on Marshall to withhold time-sensitive material that could be evidence."

Vince stared at the detective, his jaw muscles tightening. "Is that a question, Detective?"

"No, but this is. Have you been purposely interfering with a police investigation?"

Vince hesitated, weighing his response. "Detective, the news business is very competitive..."

Reggie held up his hand. "Just a yes or no, please."

"How about 'no comment'?"

"That will do." Reggie made a note, then locked eyes with Henderson. "Could you tell me where you were on Labor Day?"

Vince physically appeared to shrink away from the detective. "Are you suggesting I could have something to do with these killings?"

"I am not suggesting anything. It was merely a question."

"Why then, would you need to know?"

"You said yourself; the news business is very competitive..."

Vince was incredulous. "Are you serious?"

Reggie couldn't tell if Henderson was truly shocked or a very good actor. "Sir, it's just routine to investigate everyone connected to the case. Your news stories are definitely connected."

171

Vince's eyes narrowed. "Is this some sort of harassment for the delay in the information from Chad?"

Reggie's expression remained flat. "As I said, it's just routine."

The producer was angry now. "I was in Cedar Rapids, Iowa, visiting my brother. That's over four hours from here."

"He can verify that?"

"Of course."

"And what about the evening of September fourth?"

"Home in bed."

"Can anyone verify that?"

"No."

Reggie put away his notepad and pulled out a test kit. "I'd like to get a swab for a DNA sample."

Hostility deformed the producer's face. "Fine. I've got nothing to hide. Take your sample and then I have to get back to work."

Within thirty seconds, Reggie had completed the swab and stood up. "Thank you for your time, Mr. Henderson."

As Reggie approached the door, Vince stopped him. "Detective!"

"Yes?"

"Who do I talk with to file a complaint about harassment?"

"That would be Lieutenant Jerry Davis at the Area 5 Precinct, but Mr. Henderson…"

"What?"

"If the games you're playing with my investigation costs one young girl her life, you will come to understand what real harassment is."

Reggie walked out, leaving Henderson staring after him as he walked back down the glass hallway.

Harlem-Norwood
"L" Station
Blue Line
Norwood Park
11:15 p.m.

Gloria Hernandez pulled her curly, black hair away from her oversized hoop earrings, and wrapped an elastic band around it. Stepping off the train, she zipped up her light jacket against the evening chill, and took the stairs to street level. Waiting at the top, as promised, was her boyfriend, Marcus. He gave her a kiss and took her hand. "How was work?"

"Slow."

Gloria had taken a job four weeks earlier at La Villa, a restaurant just a ten-minute ride down the Blue Line, and ever since the death of the first girl, Marcus had met her at the train station to walk her back to campus. It was only a ten- or twelve-minute walk, but not one he wanted her making on her own until the Pledge Pin Killer was off the streets.

They walked in silence, enjoying each other's company, but both would occasionally sneak a nervous glance toward the darkness around them. Gloria felt safe with Marcus; he was a big guy who could handle himself in a fight and Marcus felt as long as he was with Gloria; she was safe.

****

He watched them from his parked car, the lights off, his outline completely hidden in the darkness. For four days now, her boyfriend had shown up to escort her, but the killer remained confident they would let their guard down. One night the boyfriend would be late, or not show at all, and the Pledge Pin Killer would have victim three.

He thought the name was kind of hokey, but it brought him the recognition he sought and served his purpose. When the couple was out of sight, he started his car and headed for home.

CHICAGO HOMICIDE

Wednesday, September 10

Home of
Sonya & Reggie Brown
Eastside Neighborhood
7:15 a.m.

Reggie was almost out the front door when the phone rang.

"Can you get that, Reggie?" Sonya called from the laundry room.

"Okay." He headed back to the kitchen and picked up. "Hello?"

"May I speak to Reggie Brown please?"

"This is Reggie Brown."

"Good morning. This is Sarah; Dr. Scott's assistant."

"Good morning."

"Mr. Brown, your surgery has been scheduled for a week from Friday. The date is September the nineteenth at eight in the morning. Will that work?"

Reggie knew Sonya was watching him. "Can you hold on?"

"Of course."

He covered the phone and turned to his wife. "They've scheduled the surgery for Friday the nineteenth at eight in the morning. Any reason we can't make it?"

"Of course not! Tell them that's fine."

"Sarah, we can make that work."

"Great. The surgeon is Dr. Carol Donahue, and her office will be in touch two days before the surgery."

"Okay. Thanks."

He hung up and turned to find Sonya writing a note on the calendar that hung on the fridge. He kissed her goodbye for the second time that morning, and headed for the precinct.

Homicide Squad Room
Area 5 Precinct
8:30 a.m.

On the way home the previous night, Reggie had dropped off the DNA swab he'd obtained from Vince Henderson. When he got to his desk this morning, two notes were waiting for him. The first was from the forensic lab.

Testing lab is running behind. DNA sample from 9/9 will be delayed at least two days.

He hadn't expected it to be waiting for him first thing this morning, but two days meant he had to find something else to focus on. The second note was a missed call.

Please call Frank Washington at CCC.

Reggie dialed the number.

The now-familiar voice of the receptionist greeted him. "Central College Security."

"Is Frank Washington in, please?"

"Who may I say is calling?"

"Detective Brown."

"Please hold, Detective."

A moment later, Frank came on. "Reggie! Thanks for calling me back."

"Of course, Frank. What's up?"

"I was calling about that knife you took for testing."

"What about it?"

"Did you get anything from it?"

"Not much of use. It had been wiped clean of prints."

"Really?"

Still bothered by the fact, Reggie probed the security chief. "Any idea why the knife would be wiped?"

"Not a clue; maybe it was accidental."

"Maybe."

"What about DNA? Get anything on that front?"

"The lab did get a sample, but it wasn't Tucker's, nor did it match our suspect DNA profile."

"Huh, that's too bad. Listen, Reggie, I need to get the knife back if you're done with it."

Reggie didn't hide his surprise. "Really? Why?"

"Well, just in case Tucker comes after it. He is entitled to have it back."

Reggie tried to think of a reason to hold on to the knife, but it wasn't tied to his case in any meaningful way, and therefore he had no grounds to keep it. Still, he wasn't going to make it easy. "That's fine, Frank. You can pick it up at the evidence locker next time you're in the area."

There was a moment's hesitation. "Oh… okay. Thanks, Reggie."

"No problem. Any new developments there?"

"Not really. Quite a few students have gone home until this blows over, but that's about it."

"I guess I can't blame them. Let me know if you need anything else."

"Will do. Bye, Reggie."

Reggie wasn't sure if there was something suspicious about Frank's behavior or he was just seeing a suspect behind every bush. Without anything else to focus on, he opted to reexamine the phone records. Maybe he could find something hiding behind one of those bushes.

****

Three hours later, Reggie had again combed all the phone records in the case file. Like before, he came away with nothing but the nagging sense he was missing something.

Someone tapped him on the shoulder. "Hey, Reggie."

He turned to find Jerry smiling down at him. "Hey, Lieutenant."

"Here's your latest phone record."

Reggie scanned it. One call was the extent of the record, the same as the other throwaways that they'd checked. This time the call pinged a tower in the center of the Loop, the very heart of the city's business

181

and government. He snorted and threw it down on the desk. "Maybe it was somebody at city hall that tipped off Marshall, ya think?"

Jerry laughed. "Lots of shady characters down there!"

"That's what I was thinking."

"You got anything going right now?"

Reggie shrugged. "I'm afraid not. Why?"

"I was thinking of grabbing a bite at Marco's. Care to come along?"

"Sounds good. You driving?"

"Not only am I driving, but I'm buying."

"That's a deal I can't refuse. Let's go."

Marco's Beef & Pizza West Fullerton Avenue 12:15 p.m.

Just five minutes from the precinct, Marco's sat on the east end of a small strip mall. Sandwiches, wings, and broasted chicken, were part of its claim to fame, and it was a favorite haunt for the officers of the Area 5 precinct.

Reggie and Jerry got their food and grabbed a table by the window. Reggie lifted his soda cup to his lieutenant. "Thanks for lunch."

"You're welcome. In another few days, you'll have to take time out from leisure living to come buy me lunch."

They ate in silence for a few minutes, Jerry studying his friend. "You never told me why you needed to take off for home on Monday."

Reggie used a napkin to wipe some sauce from his chin. "It had to do with a test result."

"Why kind of test?"

"Skin cancer biopsy."

Jerry froze, his cup halfway to his mouth. "Skin cancer?"

"Yeah. Remember that spot on my neck that was bleeding the other day?"

"Sure."

"It turned out to be cancerous."

"What kind?"

"Basal cell."

Relief unstuck the lieutenant and he finished the process of sipping his soda. "That's better than melanoma."

"You're right about that. How do you know about melanoma?"

"My brother lost his wife to it; that's scary stuff. What are they doing?"

183

"Surgery is scheduled for a week from Friday."

"Good. How is Sonya taking it?"

"She was pretty scared at first, but when the biopsy result came back, she settled down some."

Reggie had refilled his soda, and when he returned, Jerry was studying him with a solemn face. "What is it, Jerry?"

Jerry sighed. "Your case. I'm trying to decide who to pass it on to after you're gone. Do you have any thoughts on that?"

"Just one; don't be so quick to shuffle me off to the rocking chair."

"Oh? I just assumed Sonya would be ready to cuff you to keep you from working past the fifteenth."

Reggie laughed. "You may be right, but we talked about it. I think she'll be flexible if we're close to getting this guy."

"I'm glad to hear that, but *are* we close?"

Reggie shook his head. "Hardly."

"Has anything new developed?"

"A general description from one witness, but the truth is we really need a break of some sort."

"I'd hate to see your last case go cold, Reg."

"You and me both."

Harlem-Norwood
"L" Station
Blue Line
Norwood Park
11:00 p.m.

Gloria stepped off the train and made her way to the street. Earlier than normal, she'd sent a text message to Marcus to hurry up. He'd texted back that he'd be waiting, but she didn't see him anywhere. She sent another message from inside the station's glass enclosure.

Marcus, where are you?

Several minutes passed before her phone buzzed.

On my way. Be there soon.

The break in their routine unsettled her, but she was also impatient. Tired from work and with a lot of studying to do, she wanted to get back to the dorm. She texted him.

How long?

Just leaving—ten minutes.

Ten minutes! She could be back at her dorm in ten minutes. There were a few people around and it was earlier than usual, so she sent him another message.

Walking toward you—meet you at Odell and Talcott.

Sure?

Yes.

She zipped her jacket and started across the street, her steps subconsciously quicker than normal.

****

His heart rate doubled when he saw her step off the curb and cross the street. The boyfriend wasn't with her.

Sitting up straight, he checked his mirrors, then scanned the road ahead. Still no sign of her escort. His patience had paid off.

Once she had started down Odell Avenue, the tree-lined neighborhood would present him numerous locations to ambush her. He stayed low until she passed his car, then started it. Taking a parallel street, he got ahead of her, and parked in an alley. With garrote in hand, he jogged to a large tree along her path and slid down behind it.

The neighborhood of neatly trimmed brick homes was quiet and he could hear her footsteps on the sidewalk as she approached. Coiled to strike, he let her pass by him. In a flash, the wire was around her throat, trapping her scream within her lungs.

****

Marcus leaned against the chain link fence, his jacket zipped against the chilly air, peering down Odell Avenue. Checking his phone for the tenth time, his anxiety increased as he realized Gloria was overdue to their meeting spot.

Now worried, he started walking in her direction, hoping she hadn't changed her route. As he reached the end of the road, his worry turned to panic. He texted her as he walked.

Where are you?

No response, and now he'd made it all the way to the train station.

Maybe she was trying to teach him a lesson for being late.

He sent another message.

GLORIA, this is NOT funny!

Still no answer. Now he was running, taking a different route back to their meeting place, but still no Gloria. He ran all the way to her dorm, hoping to find her sitting on her bed and laughing at him. But she was not there either.

He dialed 9-1-1.

Thursday, September 11

Home of
Sonya & Reggie Brown
Eastside Neighborhood
4:15 a.m.

The fog of sleep was slow to clear when Reggie realized Sonya was pushing his shoulder. "Reggie! Reggie!"

"What?"

"The phone!"

The ringing on the bedside table finally penetrated his drowsiness. Reaching over, he dragged the receiver to his ear. "Hello?"

"Reggie, it's Jerry."

A surge of adrenaline cleared his head. "Yeah, what's up?"

"I need you down at Central College."

He was almost afraid to ask. "Why?"

"Patrol took a missing person report on a freshman student. A search turned up no sign of her and they've requested detectives. It could be your guy."

Already sitting up and wide-awake, Reggie swore under his breath. "Who do I see?"

"Officer Reynolds is with Frank Washington. They're using the security office as a starting point for the search."

"Okay. I'm on my way."

Security Offices
Central College of Chicago
Norwood Park
5:00 a.m.

Reggie found Frank standing outside talking to a police officer. The officer saw the detective and walked toward him. "Are you Detective Brown?"

"Yes."

"I'm Officer Reynolds. I responded at eleven-thirty last night to a 9-1-1 call." The officer pointed toward a young man sitting on a bench. "Marcus Peña, age twenty-one, reported his girlfriend missing. Gloria Hernandez, age twenty, and a freshman here at CCC, had not shown up to meet him."

"Where were they supposed to meet?"

"He normally meets her at the train station but she was earlier than usual. They agreed to meet at the corner of Odell and Talcott. When she didn't show, he checked her route all the way back to the train station, then backtracked to her dorm. When he still couldn't find her, he called 9-1-1."

Reggie looked over toward the young man sitting on a bench. Worry and fear were painted on his young face, and something else, too. Guilt for not meeting her, maybe? "Have you started a neighborhood search and canvas?"

"The search is ongoing. Dispatch is sending a couple more officers to help me start knocking on doors."

"Good. Let me know if you find anything."

Reggie was on his way toward Marcus when Frank intercepted him. "You think they're connected?"

"Seems likely, but until she's found, we won't know for sure. Have you secured the girl's dorm room?"

"Yes, but I didn't see any sign she'd been there since earlier today."

"What about a photo?"

Frank produced a photo for the detective. "That's her high school graduation picture."

Reggie studied it. Her large brown eyes and curly black hair spoke to a Hispanic heritage. Reggie nodded toward the boyfriend. "Let me have a word with the kid, okay?"

Frank looked over toward Marcus, then nodded. "Sure… yeah. I'll be over here."

Reggie tucked the photo in his jacket and approached the bench. "Marcus?"

The young man looked up through bloodshot eyes. "Yeah?"

"My name is Detective Brown. May I sit down?"

"Sure." Marcus scooted to one side, even though there was plenty of room for the detective. Reggie eased down next to him, taking note of his physique. It would be easy for Marcus to control a woman.

He took out his notepad. "Where do you usually meet Gloria?"

"At the Blue Line station near Odell."

"And she was earlier than usual, is that right?"

"Yeah, about fifteen minutes. I didn't get started soon enough and she was off the train before I got there."

"Where was she coming from?"

"Work. She's a waitress at La Villa, a restaurant near the Addison station"

Reggie made a note to check the restaurant as well as the train station for video. "So, she decided not to wait for you at the station?"

"Right. She wanted to meet halfway, so I asked her if she was sure, and she insisted."

"On these walks from the station to her dorm, had you ever seen anyone watching you?"

His eyebrows spiked with surprise at the question. "No, and if I had, I would've beat the life out of him."

Reggie smiled. "I imagine you would have. Is there anywhere you can think of that she might have gone without telling you?"

Marcus shook his head, certain in his conviction. "No way! She knew I didn't want her out alone."

"Okay. As a matter of routine, I need to get a DNA swab from you. Is that okay?"

His eyes widened. "I didn't hurt Gloria!"

"I'm not accusing you of anything, Marcus. It's just something I have to do to cover all the bases, okay?"

The boy composed himself. "I guess."

"I'll have a tech come over and see you; just hang here for a few minutes."

"I've got nowhere to go until we find Gloria."

"We're gonna do all we can to locate her." He reached into his jacket and retrieved a business card. "If you hear from her or think of anything, call me."

"I will."

Reggie left the boy alone and went to find an evidence tech. Unsuccessful, he waved over to Officer Reynolds. "Yes, Detective?"

"Find a forensic tech and secure a DNA sample from Mr. Peña."

"Yes, sir."

Reggie checked his watch.

Time to wake up, Chad.

He dialed the reporter's number and got his voicemail.

"Chad, this is Reggie Brown. Call me as soon as you get this."

Reggie figured his next stop should be the headquarters of the Chicago Transit Authority, but that was at least an hour away, more if the traffic was bad. Still, the CTA video system could give him proof Gloria Hernandez got on the train, then off the train at her stop, and possibly the face of anyone who interacted with her.

He notified Frank, found Officer Reynolds and told him, then left a message for Jerry. He was on the road toward downtown by six.

Headquarters
Chicago Transit Authority
West Lake Street
7:15 a.m.

While traffic hadn't been terrible, it was bad enough to add twenty minutes to his drive. The CTA office was just west of where the Chicago River split into the north and south branches. A gleaming, twelve-story silver and teal office complex, it was the hub of CTA business.

Reggie had been down there many times for the exact same reason. CTA video was an invaluable resource for police work in the city. Nearly one thousand arrests had been made with the help of their camera system. Reggie was hoping to make it a thousand and one.

The new video surveillance room was nearly twenty-eight-hundred square feet of technology, with both live and recorded feeds that could be accessed to help first responders, CTA security, and Chicago PD.

It was literally humming with activity when he entered.

"Reggie!"

Bryan Mercer, a lanky man who had semi-pro basketball in his past, had helped Reggie on other cases. "Bryan, long time. How are you?"

"Not as good as you. I heard you're giving up the rat race to lay on a beach somewhere."

Reggie laughed. "I'm not sure I can afford a beach, but maybe a nice easy chair."

"Good for you. What brings you down here?"

"You've heard about the Central College murders?"

The smile left Bryan's face. "Yeah, sure. The Pledge Pin thing?"

"That's the one. I'm working the case and looking for a girl who rode your trains last night."

"Okay, which line?"

"Blue Line from Addison to Harlem-Norwood."

"What time?"

"She apparently got off at Harlem just about eleven."

"Follow me."

Bryan led him on a winding trail through the banks of monitors and screens that reminded Reggie of Mission Control at

196

NASA. Stopping at a desk in the back corner, Bryan punched some keys and spun a knob, quickly producing an in-station camera view.

"This is the Addison station at ten forty-five." The picture scrolled forward, and after just a minute, Reggie pointed at the screen. "That's her."

Immediately, a train pulled in and they watched as Gloria got on. So far, she hadn't talked to anyone. Bryan switched to the live camera inside the train, finding the car containing the girl. She had sat alone, listening to her headphones. Bryan narrated as the film moved forward.

"The next station is Irving Park, followed by Montrose, and then Jefferson Park."

They watched as the train pulled into and back out of all three stations. Several people got on and off, but no one interacted with their girl, and she appeared unconcerned by her surroundings.

"Okay, here we come into Harlem."

Gloria stood, faced the door, and waited for the train to stop. Getting off, she turned toward the stairs. Bryan flipped to the platform camera and they followed Gloria up the stairs until she was out of sight. She was not followed.

Reggie sighed. "What time was that?"

"Eleven-oh-one."

"Can I get a copy?"

"Of course. I'll be right back."

While he was waiting, Reggie's phone rang. "Detective Brown."

"Detective, this is Chad Marshall."

"Yes, Chad. Thanks for calling…"

"I got another message."

Reggie's heart sunk. "A body?"

"Yes. It was on my phone right before your message."

"Where?"

"White Eagle Woods; you know it?"

"Sort of."

"There's a park entrance off Fortieth Street; she's supposed to be at the end of the road."

"Are you there?"

"On my way."

"Me too."

White Eagle Woods
South Picnic Grove
8:00 a.m.

Reggie had called in the crime scene and patrol had arrived before Chad. The

198

reporter stood with Vince and a cameraman on the outside of yellow crime tape, trying to get information from the officer who was holding them at bay. Their news truck was parked next to the coroner's van.

Reggie came up behind the group, showing his badge to the officer. "Is the scene secure?"

"Yes, sir. Coroner Thorsen is already back there."

Reggie turned to Chad. "Did you get any shots of the scene?"

"No!" Vince answered for his reporter.

The cameraman apparently shared his producer's frustration. "It wasn't for lack of trying!"

Reggie sized him up. "Who's this, Chad?"

"Tommy Castillo; he's the third member of our team. Tommy, this is Detective Brown."

"Charmed."

Reggie noted Castillo was Hispanic. "Equally glad to meet you, Mr. Castillo. We should have a chat soon."

"Why?"

Reggie dipped under the yellow tape and moved down the path, leaving the question unanswered. The sign where the pavement stopped read DEAD END, striking Reggie as both ironic and prophetic.

199

Beyond the sign, tall grasses fed around to the right and butted up against a tree line. That was where he found Thorsen and her team.

"Hey, Janet."

The coroner, bent over and peering at the girl's face, straightened up when she heard the detective's voice. "Hey, Reggie."

To the detective, the scene resembled both the previous ones, with the exception of water. The nearest river was more than a hundred yards away, but Zoo Woods was just over a mile from where they stood.

The victim matched the photo of Gloria Hernandez, turning the girl's case from a missing person to homicide. And her missing underwear combined with the bruising to the throat told him it was the same killer. "Did you check the mouth, Doc?"

"Not yet." Thorsen went down on one knee, and with some effort, pried open the mouth. Using a pair of forceps, she removed a pin. She held it out to Reggie. "It's similar to one of the previous cases, isn't it?"

Reggie nodded. "Victim two, Gina Montrose; Kappa Gamma Phi."

Thorsen dropped it into an evidence bag. "Do the girls have to wear these all the time?"

"I'm not sure. Why?"

"Because she's in her work uniform."

Reggie reached over and pulled down the girl's shirt. "I don't see where it's been torn loose from her clothes." He looked around the scene. "Did they find any of her stuff?"

"Her purse was found in the grass over there."

"Where?"

She pointed. "The photographer's shooting it now."

Reggie spotted the forensic photographer about thirty yards deeper into the woods and walked over. "You almost done?"

The young woman nodded. "Just a couple more."

After just thirty seconds, she nodded at the detective and moved off. Reggie bent over and, using a pen, exposed the empty interior of the purse. Probably dumped while searching for something, and since none of the previous two scenes involved robbery, it figured the purse is where the pin came from.

When Reggie returned to where the body lay, Janet was writing down some observations in a notebook. She paused to look at him. "How did it come out?"

"How did what come out?"

"The biopsy?"

Reggie eyebrows spiked upward. "How did you know?"

She shrugged. "Things get around."

"It came back positive for cancer."

She averted her eyes. "What kind?"

"*Nasal* cell carcinoma."

"I see."

Reggie watched in amazement as a smile curled slowly across her face. "Are you smiling, Doc?"

She laughed. "Yes, but not because you have nose cell cancer!"

Reggie grinned. "Oh, come on. That was funny!"

"If you say so, but I'm smiling because *basal* cell means you're not going to die!"

Reggie was touched by her concern. "Thanks, Doc." He turned back to the victim. "When do you think you'll do the autopsy?"

"First thing tomorrow."

"Okay."

Reggie took a last look around and then made his way back to the road. Several other news teams had joined Chad, Vince, and Tommy. Reggie waved for Chad to come over to the crime tape. Several others followed, calling out random questions, but they didn't have what the detective wanted. "I'll give a statement in a minute; right now I have some questions for Mr. Marshall."

He lifted the tape and allowed Chad to duck underneath and join him inside the scene. Taking him about twenty feet from the tape, he kept his voice low. "You have a copy of the message for me?"

"Yeah." Chad handed the flash drive over. "Can you give me something?"

Reggie pondered the question. He didn't want to compromise the investigation any more than it already had been. "What do you want to know?"

"Was there a pledge pin in her throat?"

Reggie paused. "Let's just say that the crime scene matches the two previous ones."

"What sorority was the pin from?"

"No comment."

"What about the underwear?"

"Let's just say that the crime scene matches the two previous ones."

"What was the cause of death?"

"Let's just say that the crime scene matches the two previous ones." Reggie nodded toward the crime tape. "Back on the other side, Chad."

After steering the reporter back out of the scene, Reggie stepped under himself and started for his car. A crowd of reporters followed, so upon reaching his vehicle, he turned to face them.

"I can confirm that another body has been found. At this time, I'm not at liberty to release the identity of the victim, nor any other information. There will be another statement made after the autopsy is completed."

Someone in the back called out. "When will that be?"

"Sometime tomorrow morning."

With that, Reggie ducked into his vehicle and started it up. Within seconds, he'd left the reporters behind and headed for the precinct.

Homicide Squad Room Area 5 Precinct 10:00 a.m.

When Reggie got back to his desk, he found a manila folder marked *Neighborhood Canvas*. Inside were nearly two dozen sheets of paper filled out by officers who had banged on doors near where Gloria went missing.

The majority of the sheets were near duplicates of each other. The first line listed the officer's name, followed by the time, the address, the person's name if someone answered the door, and then a final comment: *Did not see anything unusual.*

One page stood out above the rest; Officer Reynolds had interviewed a Mr. Thomas Kane of Octavia Avenue.

Mr. Kane reported he was walking his dog just after eleven last night when he noticed a man walking along West Ardmore dressed in a hoodie and jeans. The man was on the opposite side of the street from Mr. Kane, but they did exchange looks, and Mr. Kane could not recall ever seeing the man in the neighborhood before.

Mr. Kane said he did not see the man enter or exit a vehicle, and he lost sight of the man after turning down his street toward his home. He gave the basic description of a black or Hispanic male, five-foot-ten, approximately one hundred seventy pounds.

I asked Mr. Kane if he thought he could describe the individual to a sketch artist, he was unsure, but agreed to try.

"Reggie?"

He looked over his shoulder. "Yes, sir?"

"Come in here, will ya?"

"Of course." Reggie went into the lieutenant's office and closed the door behind him. Jerry pointed at the report Reggie still carried. "I saw that. We have a sketch artist meeting with Thomas Kane later this afternoon."

"Excellent."

Jerry fell into his chair and let out a sigh. "I gather we have another one?"

"I'm afraid so. Everything matches the previous two scenes."

"Same college?"

"Yes, but this time, the pledge is also from the same sorority as victim two."

"Has the family been notified?"

"I called Frank at CCC when I left Eagle Woods. He said the parents live out of state and he would handle the notification."

"Find anything at the scene to help?"

"Not really. They're just dumpsites. I don't think the killer is there more than a couple minutes."

"Alright, if the sketch is decent, let's get it on the news tonight."

"I'll fax it to all the outlets as soon as it's done. I'm also going to run it past our witness from Salt Creek. By the way, I need the phone records from the latest message to Marshall." Reggie dropped the number on the desk.

"Did you listen to it?"

"Yes. It sounds just like the rest."

"Okay, I'll file the subpoena before meeting with the chief. He wants twice daily updates now."

"Good luck with that."
"Thanks, I'll need it."

Interview Room
Area 5 Precinct
3:30 p.m.

Reggie had wanted to sit in on the sketch session with Mr. Kane, but the department artist felt it would distract the man. So he'd spent the last hour staring through the one-way glass as the drawing took shape. Using photos of different facial features, first several pages of head shapes, then several pages of hairstyles, the sketch started to come together. The artist then had Kane select from multiple noses, eyes, lips and chins, which he drew into the image.

When he had all the parts in place, he added a hoodie to the outside of the man's head, then held it up for Kane to see. "Does this look like the man you saw?"

Kane stared at it, then nodded. "Pretty much. Like I said, it was dark and we only looked at each other briefly."

The artist waved Reggie in. "Here it is."

Reggie held it up and studied it. "This man is African-American. You originally thought he could be Hispanic, correct?"

Kane shrugged. "True, but that looks like him."

"Okay, Mr. Kane. Thank you so much."

"You're welcome. I hope it helps."

After Reggie had multiple copies printed off and faxed to all the local news organizations, he headed for Jackson Avenue with his own copy.

Home of
Mrs. Stella Esposito
Jackson Avenue
4:45 p.m.

Reggie stopped in front of the small white house and put his vehicle in park. Grabbing the sketch off the seat next to him, he stepped out to hear his name. "Come back after that rain check, Reggie?"

Stella sat moving back and forth on her porch glider. He waved. "Is the rain check still good?"

"Most definitely."

"Then yes, I'm here to collect."

He came on to the porch just as she stood, a wide grin on her face. "Nice to see you again, Reggie." She disappeared into the house and returned a few minutes later with two glasses of iced tea. Reggie accepted his and drank deeply. "This was well worth the trip, Stella."

She smiled, accepting the compliment graciously. "Nice of you to say so. I make sun tea; do you know what that is, Reggie?"

"I do. You put it in a large jar and place it in the direct sunshine. My grandmother used to make it that way."

She sipped hers. "I think it gives the tea a little something special."

She placed her glass on the table next to her, folded her hands in her lap, and resumed her gliding. "Well, despite your claim, I believe you came all the way over here for something other than my tea. What can I do for you?"

He smiled. "I have a sketch for you to look at. Do you mind?"

"Not at all. Is that it?"

"Yes." Reggie set his own glass down and handed the drawing to Stella. She stared at it for nearly a minute, then reached up and slid her glasses down from on her head, before taking another full minute to look at the drawing.

Finally, she handed it back. "It could be him, but in all honesty, he was pretty far away for these old eyes."

"But it *could* be him?"

"Sure, it could be, but look at the sketch yourself, Reggie. There's absolutely nothing distinctive about the drawing. It could be you!"

He looked at the picture again, and he had to admit she was right. There was nothing distinguishing about the drawing, and they weren't even positive they had the correct racial coloring.

She was watching him. "I'm right, aren't I?"

He nodded. "I can't argue with you."

"Good thing too; you'd lose!"

He laughed. "I have no doubt. Can I get a refill on my tea?"

"You certainly can. Right through that door and into the kitchen."

He stood. "How about you?"

"I'm fine, thank you. Just fine."

*Home of
Sonya & Reggie Brown
Eastside Neighborhood
6:30 p.m.*

Reggie and Sonya watched the news together with dinner in their laps. The sketch was featured on all the newscasts, and Reggie hoped the drawing struck a chord with someone in the city. What he expected would happen was every nut in town would think the generic sketch was their crazy relative, and the hotline would be inundated with leads that went nowhere.

He looked over at Sonya after she saw the drawing for the third time. "Does he look familiar to you, Honey?"

She laughed. "Yeah. He looks a little like you in a hoodie!"

Reggie groaned. "I was afraid of that."

Friday, September 12

Homicide Squad Room
Area 5 Precinct
8:15 a.m.

Reggie arrived to find a pile of leads on his desk. A quick scan revealed his worst fear. Calls had poured in from every corner of the city as well as the surrounding counties. Going through them would be a monumental task, one he didn't have time to do.

"Detective Brown?"

Reggie looked up to see an unfamiliar face. "Yes?"

"I'm Detective Wallace."

"Nice to meet you, Wallace. What can I do for you?"

"I'm the one Lieutenant Davis told you about."

Reggie's blank stare elicited an awkward smile from the young man. "Or… maybe I'm the one he *didn't* tell you about."

"I'm sorry, but I'm afraid I'm in the dark."

The young detective, less than half Reggie's age, managed a laugh. "Lieutenant Davis asked me to go through the calls that came in to the tip line last night."

"The tip line… Oh, you mean these!" He held the pile out to Wallace.

The young man took the stack, surprised at the weight. "Wow, there are a lot of them."

"You can set up in the conference room."

"Okay. What are we looking for?"

"Try to thin the pile to leads that have some credibility to them. Look for tips that give a name, not just references like my jerk neighbor or shady co-worker. Then call the lead back and see if they give you more to go on than just the similarity to the sketch."

"Got it."

"Call me if you have any questions about the responses or tips."

"I will." As Wallace walked away, Reggie was suddenly curious. "Hey, Wallace."

"Yeah?"

"Have we met before?"

"No, sir. I've been working property crimes in Area 4."

"Well, thanks for the help. I appreciate it a lot."

Wallace grinned. "Save your thanks until after I'm done. That's when we'll know if I've been any help."

Reggie laughed, then looked toward Jerry's office. It was still empty.

I owe you a big thanks, Jerry!

Turning back to his desk, he noticed that the pile of phone leads had been covering up another piece of paper. The phone record from the killer's call about victim three. He picked it up and scanned it.

Not surprisingly, the call was made from a popular location. This time, it pinged a tower near Soldier Field, possibly from Burnham Harbor. That narrowed it down to about a thousand boats, a giant park, and an immense stadium. Their killer was not taking any chances, and as a result, not giving Reggie much to go on.

He added the report to the others in his file just as his phone started to ring.

"Homicide; Brown."

"Reggie, this is Janet."

"Hi, Doc. You done with the Hernandez girl's autopsy?"

"As a matter of fact, yes."

"And?"

"Time of death was between midnight and six in the morning."

"Manner of death match?"

"It did. Strangulation, likely the double-loop garrote."

Reggie sensed his blood pressure climbing. "Trace evidence?"

"Afraid not. No rape kit needed, either."

Reggie sighed. "Okay, Doc. Send me the report as soon as you can."

"Hold on a second, Reg."

His heart skipped a beat. "Got something else?"

"I do. Beneath the girl's hairline, on the back of her neck, was a large smudge of something. At first, I thought it was dirt, but then I swabbed it with a cotton ball."

"Not mud?"

"Nope. What it turned out to be was really strange."

"Come on, Doc; throw me a bone, please!"

The coroner laughed. "The smudge turned out to be a make-up compound."

Reggie, who had his pen poised over his notepad, closed his eyes. "Make-up? That's not a big surprise on a female victim!"

"Reggie, you wound me. I know that isn't a big deal, but this was not cosmetic make-up; this was black stage make-up."

Reggie let it roll around in his head for a minute. "Stage make-up? Like for theater productions and that sort of thing?"

"Precisely."

"So, our killer was possibly wearing it to disguise his skin color?"

"Possibly, or to take any shine off his face. However, because this was near where the garrote would have been tightened, I'm inclined to think it came from his hands."

"But we believe our killer has been wearing gloves."

"True, but what if he put the make-up on with his gloves?"

"Possible, I guess. If it was in contact with his skin, can you get DNA?"

"I'm sending it off for testing but I doubt it. The chemicals in the make-up would almost certainly destroy the perp's skin oils."

"Is there any way to identify the particular brand?"

"Not likely, but I can tell you it has a wax base and is water activated. I tested a small sample for its chemical properties."

Reggie was now in full investigative mode, thinking of all the avenues he could use to track down the substance. "Anything else, Doc?"

"Not now. I'll let you know if the DNA test shows anything."

"Good. Thanks for the call."

Reggie hung up and turned on his computer. Doing a Google search for black stage make-up, he discovered it could be ordered from dozens of places online, but he suspected his killer wanted to pay cash. That meant going to a local store, and just seven locations listed the product in their inventory. Reggie printed off the list and headed for the parking lot.

Home of
Sonya & Reggie Brown
Eastside Neighborhood
7:00 p.m.

By the time Reggie headed for home, he'd visited four of the seven make-up shops on his list. Two were out because it was on backorder, one hadn't sold it in over a year, and the other shop had closed its doors two months before. With the other three probably closed for the day, he made it home in time for a late dinner with Sonya.

Afterwards, they sat quietly on the back deck sipping coffee. Finally, Sonya asked the question constantly on her mind these days. "How's the case going?"

Reggie shrugged. "So-so. I have a lead I'm working, but if it doesn't pan out, I don't know where I'll go next."

"Monday is coming, you know."

He smiled. "I know; I haven't forgotten."

She touched his hand. "I'm not trying to be difficult, Reggie."

"I know you're not, and I'm a lucky man to have you. Most guys' wives hope they'll prolong their career and stay out of their hair!"

She laughed. "Well, not that I haven't thought about it, but I'll take my chances with having you around."

"Good, because the reality is you don't have a choice!"

<u>Saturday, September 13</u>

Homicide Squad Room
Area 5 Precinct
7:45 a.m.

Taped to the computer monitor on his desk, Reggie found a note from Detective Wallace.

Detective Brown,

I am still working my way through the leads, but this one seemed different. The caller referred us to a news report done by Chad Marshall at his previous job.
The station is an ABC affiliate in Sioux Falls, South Dakota — WWSD. You can find the stories on their website.

Wallace

Reggie pulled the note off his monitor and fired up the computer. Searching for WWSD, he was redirected to their website, where he clicked on the tab *News Archives.* The first story to pop up was about the kidnapping of an eight-year-old girl. Chad was standing in front of a rural home surrounded by yellow tape, speaking into a mic. Reggie put the report in motion.

This is Chad Marshall at the home of Bill and Mary Dyson. Earlier today, their eight-year-old daughter Desiree was discovered missing. This reporter, who had received a note through his mail slot from the kidnapper, had alerted police to the situation.
The Dysons were not aware of the situation until Sheriff Nick Pointer knocked on the door, and asked them to check the girl's bedroom.

Reggie stopped the playback and tried to catch his breath. A kidnapper had contacted Marshall at his previous job with information about a crime. Reggie didn't know what the odds against such a thing were, but it happening twice must be astronomical. Chad Marshall was either the luckiest newsman in the business, or an accessory to the crimes themselves.

Reggie replayed the video, this time writing down the sheriff's name. Punching the name into a Google search, he got a hit for the Lincoln County Sheriff's office in South Sioux Falls. He dialed the number, and after just two rings, a female voice picked up.

"Lincoln County Sheriff's Department."

"Yes, is Sheriff Pointer in?"

"May I ask who's calling?"

"My name is Detective Brown with the Chicago Police Department."

"Very well; please hold."

Less than a minute later, the strong and deep voice of Sheriff Nick Pointer came on the line. "This is Sheriff Pointer."

"Hi, Sheriff. My name is Reggie Brown with the Chicago PD—Homicide bureau."

"Good morning, Detective. What can those of us in Sioux Falls do for you big city boys?"

Reggie laughed. "I'm calling in reference to a case you had earlier this year."

"Which case?"

"The kidnapping of an eight-year-old girl."

The humor instantly left the sheriff's voice. "That was a scary time around these parts."

"What was the outcome?"

"She was returned to her family after four days, uninjured and healthy."

Reggie was making notes. "No assault of any kind?"

"Nope. She said the man treated her nicely, even bringing her ice cream."

"Did you catch the guy?"

"Not yet. Unfortunately, the case has gone cold. I haven't had a new lead in over two months."

"What was the motive, do you know?"

"A ransom note was delivered to a reporter, but it was an amount far beyond the ability of the Dysons to pay."

"The reporter, was it Chad Marshall?"

"Yeah, how did you know?"

"I'm investigating a series of homicides and he is similarly involved."

"Similarly how?"

"He's been receiving phone messages from the killer."

There was a moment of silence on the other end of the phone. Finally, the sheriff found his voice. "You're joking!"

"I'm not."

"Well, slap me silly. That is one peculiar occurrence, don't you think?"

"Seems so to me. Was Marshall ever a suspect?"

"No. I checked him out, but he had an alibi for the morning it happened, and he was very helpful with the case."

"Was the little girl able to give you a description of her captor?"

"Not really; whenever they interacted, either she was blindfolded or he had a mask on."

"Would you mind sending me the basic outline of the case file?"

"Not at all. Where to?"

Reggie gave him the station's fax number.

"I'll send it within the hour."

"Thanks, I appreciate it."

"Sure, but if your case pegs him as being involved, let me know, will ya?"

"You'll be the first."

****

An hour later, Reggie was sitting in his lieutenant's office holding the case outline from South Dakota. On Jerry's laptop, the same report Reggie had watched was playing back for his boss. Reggie looked on as the surprise registered on his boss's face. When the report was over, Jerry leaned back in his chair. "That's incredible."

"Seems a little too far-fetched to think he was that lucky twice in a row."

"I'll say. What's your next step?"

"I want to subpoena his phone records. It's time to take a closer look at Chad Marshall."

"I'll file the request today, but it will likely be Monday morning before you get a response."

"I figured."

The phone on Reggie's desk started to ring. He got up and answered it. "Homicide; Brown."

"Hey, Reggie. It's Janet."

"Hi, Doc."

"I just got the DNA back on the Vince Henderson. It's not a match to the fingernails of victim one."

"I guess I'm not surprised, considering the smudge you found on the Hernandez girl."

"I was thinking the same thing."

"Thanks, Janet."

"At your service, Reggie."

He smiled. "Tell you what, why don't you take the rest of the weekend off?"

She laughed. "Why don't I, indeed?"

Sunday, September 14

Home of
Sonya & Reggie Brown
Eastside Neighborhood
11:30 a.m.

Instead of going out to lunch after church, their usual Sunday routine, Sonya and Reggie came home. The weather was warm and the leaves on the trees in their backyard were turning multiple colors of reds and golds. With bowls of soup and crackers, they sat on the back porch enjoying each other's company.

Reggie's thoughts bounced back and forth. First, to how nice it will be when they have the freedom to do this kind of thing all the time. Then to the pledge pin case, which he wanted to solve soon so they *could* do this all the time.

Sonya smiled at him. "Penny for your thoughts, although I think I know what they are."

He returned her smile. "Just thinking how nice this is."

"How about the case? Thinking about it too?"

"You know me; it's hard to leave work behind."

"Is the case progressing?"

"It is; my feeling is I'm getting close."

"Good."

"It's unlikely I'll have it all put together by Monday night, though."

Again, she smiled, this time a knowing glint in her eyes. "I have no doubt you'll catch him, and if it takes a few days more, I'll survive."

He leaned over and kissed her. "You keep showing me more and more reasons why I'm the luckiest man on Earth."

"Besides, there's a deadline I have nothing to do with."

He nodded. "I can't argue with that."

The Friday deadline was a line in the sand. Solved or not, he had to have the surgery, and there would be no returning to work if the operation revealed the cancer was deeper than they anticipated.

The ringing phone pierced the quiet of their backyard lunch. Sonya stood and grabbed their plates. "I'll get it. I imagine that's Nina."

Campus Library
Central College of Chicago
Norwood Park
11:15 p.m.

Caitlin Butler finished taking notes from the reference book in front of her, closing the thick volume with a thud. Rubbing her eyes, she looked across the table at her friend. "Sam, are you about done?"

Samantha Blevins nodded and closed her own notebook. "I am *so* done!"

"Good. Let's get outta here. I'm beat."

They returned the reference books, gathered up their belongings, and walked outside. The evening was cool, but not uncomfortable, and they stayed on the lighted path as they moved toward Hammond Hall. The entire student body at CCC had been warned not to walk alone, either on or off the college's campus, and to avoid dark places where an attacker could hide.

Caitlin had not wanted to come back to school so quickly, but she couldn't afford to miss the classes. It had helped when Samantha agreed to become her roommate.

Together, they'd made every effort to be safe and watch out for each other.

Sam sighed. "I need to do this all over again tomorrow night. What about you?"

"I don't have to use the library, but if you're going, I can do my studying there too."

"Awesome."

Caitlin rubbed her arms, trying to banish her goosebumps. Unsure if it was the cold, or the sense they were being watched that chilled her, she eventually decided the breeze was the cause of her discomfort.

Since returning to school, neither girl had left the CCC campus. In Caitlin's case, promising to stay on college grounds was the only way she convinced her mother to let her come back; that along with the phone calls. Every night, Caitlin called her mother to report she was safe in her dorm, regardless of how late the hour, and her mother always picked up on the first ring. Caitlin had joked with Sam that her mother must have been circling the phone like a hawk.

The walk from the library on the northeast corner of the campus to their dorm hall was less than ten minutes. It was uneventful, just like they hoped.

****

Parked in his darkened car, across the street from the northeast corner of CCC, he watched them study. The bright lights and large windows of the campus library made it easy. Not long after eleven, they packed up and came outside. From his vantage point, he could watch their progress across the campus toward Hammond Hall.

Caitlin Butler, the former roommate of his first victim, would be perfect for his fourth kill. It would bring things full circle before he moved away, and should help confuse the investigation because of the girls' connection to each other.

Caitlin and her friend had been coming to the library every night since she returned to school, and a regular schedule was the thing he needed most to do his planning.

It wouldn't be long now; he could feel it.

A set of lights lit up his rearview mirror, and he quickly slid lower in his seat. Moving down the road at a crawl was a campus security vehicle. At each parked car, a bright spotlight searched back and forth through the window.

Judging it too risky to pull out and leave, he pressed himself to the seat, forcing his head below the edge of the glass. Within moments, the spotlight lit up the interior of his car. His heart pounded as he stared at his shoes, now illuminated by the spotlight. After what seemed like an eternity, the light flicked off and the officer's car moved on to the next one in line.

The killer, unaware he'd been holding his breath, exhaled loudly. Sucking in fresh oxygen, he tried to slow his pulse. He'd never come so close to being caught, and it unnerved him.

But there was no turning back.

Caitlin was the last; killing her would complete his mission. He waited a full ten minutes longer, well after the officer rounded the corner at the far end of the block, before starting his car and leaving.

Despite the close call, he would be back again tomorrow night.

Monday, September 15

Homicide Squad Room
Area 5 Precinct
8:15 a.m.

Sonya had made him his to-go cup of coffee, kissed his cheek, then sent him off as if it were any other day. She never mentioned the fact it was supposed to be his retirement day.

The opposite was true when he arrived at the precinct. There was a box of donuts on his desk with a note. "We're gonna miss you, but at least there will be donuts left for the rest of us once you're gone!"

It wasn't signed, but Reggie had a pretty good idea who left it. He picked up the box and carried it to the lieutenant's office. "Jerry, you want a donut before I eat them all?"

Davis laughed. "Don't mind if I do."

Reggie set the box on Jerry's desk. "Am I going to get a new box every day until I'm outta here?"

"I thought that day was today."

"I've been granted a reprieve by the queen. She knows I want to solve this case."

"Well, I for one, am glad. How long is this reprieve you refer to?"

"Until Friday."

"That's right; you have the surgery on Friday, don't you?"

"Yeah."

Jerry grabbed a second donut. "Well then, what about this case. You got any ideas?"

"Yeah, I'm waiting on those phone records."

"They should be here around lunchtime, I think."

"Good. I'm going to pair them with the records from the throwaway phones. Laying each day of Chad's record next to the throwaways from the same day. I'm hoping to find a hole in his story somewhere on those pages."

Jerry polished off his second donut, then swallowed hard. "I like it. Maybe you can prove he wasn't just lucky to get his inside information, but had somebody feeding it to him."

The phone on Reggie's desk started ringing. Still standing, it was just three steps for the big man to reach the call. "Homicide; Detective Brown."

"Hey Reggie, it's Janet. I guess today's the big day, huh?"

"Not yet. I've got a few days' grace to catch the animal who's killing these college girls."

"Great. I wish I could help, but I've got another dead end for you. The DNA from Marcus Peña was not a match to our perp."

"I'm not surprised, I guess. I couldn't find where he had a connection to either of the other two victims."

"Let me know if you need anything else. Good luck."

"Thanks, Doc."

****

Just past ten-thirty, the phone records landed on his desk with a thud. The thick sheaf of paper contained the last thirty days of Chad Marshall's phone activity, and he was a man who was on the phone a lot. Reggie gathered up the pile and moved directly to the conference room.

After spreading the papers out on the long table, then sorting them by date, he returned to his desk for the throwaway phone records. On each of the days when the killer called Chad, Reggie paired up the phone records, then set them aside for further study.

Once he had all of Chad's incoming records paired with the killer's outgoing calls, he went in search of a yellow highlighter and more coffee. Having secured both, he sequestered himself in the conference room with the door closed.

Starting with the first call on September second, and continuing with each call since, he highlighted five times the killer and Marshall communicated. Now, he went back over the five calls, and made his own notes:

9/2 – Mackenzie Addison location – Call pinged from Grant Park
9/4 – Warning of victim #2 – Call pinged from Navy Pier
9/5 – Gina Montrose location – Call pinged from Navy Pier
9/8 – Pins in mouths revealed – Call pinged from Chicago Loop
9/11 – Gloria Hernandez location – Call pinged from Soldier Field

Next, Reggie started looking at what towers had pinged the incoming calls to Chad's phone. He thought his head would explode as he wrote next to each of his previous notes.

9/2 – Mackenzie Addison location – call pinged from Grant Park — *Grant Pk.*

9/4 – Warning of victim #2 – Call pinged from Navy Pier — *Navy Pr.*

9/5 – Gina Montrose location – Call pinged from Navy Pier — *Navy Pr.*

9/8 – Pins in mouth revealed – Call pinged from Chicago Loop — *Loop*

9/11 – Gloria Hernandez location – Call pinged from Soldier Field — *Soldier Fd.*

Either Chad Marshall was sitting next to the killer and getting information, or Chad Marshall *was* the killer. Reggie's head spun.

What would be the motive? Not just a news story?

He studied his other notes and realized he'd never confirmed Chad's alibi. His confidence shaken, he fought the idea of making this his last day after all. If it was Chad, why didn't he see it before? He checked his notes.

Christie Shaw – Shriner's Hospital for Children.

Grabbing a blank piece of paper, he scribbled *please do not disturb* across it, then taped it to the outside of the conference room door. Five minutes later, he was on his way to the Shriner's Hospital.

Shriner's Hospital for Children
North Oak Park Avenue
1:30 p.m.

The sprawling campus of Shriner's Hospital was in the northwest section of the city. Glass arches and brightly colored tables highlighted the reddish brick structure. A beehive of activity, Reggie arrived to find his only option for a parking spot was a long hike from the front door.

Once inside the front lobby, a friendly face greeted him, eager to help. "Good afternoon. Welcome to Shriner's."

Reggie produced his badge. "Hi. I'm Detective Brown with Chicago PD. I'd like to speak to one of your nurses."

The young lady with a blonde, bouncy undercut and bright, blue eyes showed little reaction to the badge. "Oh, we have a lot of great nurses here, but I only know a handful of them. Perhaps you'd like to speak to our Human Resources manager?"

"That sounds like a good idea."

"Okay." She picked up the phone and connected with somebody, nodded her head, and then hung up. "Through that door over there, then down the hall to the last office on the right."

Reggie thanked her and followed her directions. A small sign hung over the door indicating he'd found his destination. Sitting at the only desk in the office was a man in his mid-fifties, neatly dressed in a suit and tie, who looked up when Reggie entered. "Detective Brown?"

"Yes, sir, but Reggie will be fine."

The man stood and extended his hand. "Rick Cooper; nice to meet you."

"Thanks for seeing me. I'm looking to speak with one of your nurses."

"What's her name?"

"Christie Shaw."

Rick sat back down at his desk. "Ah, yes, I've know her for years. She works in our burn unit. Let me see if she's here." He picked up the phone.

Just the mention of the burn unit sent an involuntary chill up Reggie's spine. He'd seen the devastation burns caused, and was inclined to respect Miss Shaw without even meeting her. Anybody who could work with kids going through such trauma, in his book, was a saint.

Rick hung up. "She's here, and since the burn unit is a sterile area, I've asked her to meet us in the lobby."

Rick stood and led the way back to the lobby. After just a few minutes, a pretty nurse wearing a pink smock covered with animal prints joined them. She had short, black hair and delicate features, which combined with an easy smile to make her very attractive. When she reached the table where the men were sitting, Rick introduced the detective.

She smiled and nodded. "Hullo."

Reggie picked up on the slight speech imperfection, noticing she focused on his lips when he spoke. "Hi, Miss Shaw. I'm sorry to pull you away from your work."

"It's fine."

"I have a few questions about your boyfriend, Chad Marshall."

"Yes, he said you might come here."

"Can you tell me where Chad was on Labor Day?"

"We took a drive up to Fox Lake and had lunch. After getting back in town, we stayed in for dinner."

"Was he with you all day?"

"Yesss."

"Do you remember what time you went to bed?"

"Around ten, I think."

Reggie noticed Christie wore hearing aids in both ears. "Forgive me Miss Shaw, I don't mean to be rude, but can I ask you about your hearing aids?"

She looked at Rick, unsure why they would be important. Rick turned to Reggie. "Christie has been partially deaf since birth. She works with kids whose hearing has been compromised by their burns."

Reggie smiled at the young nurse. "I think that's awesome; you should be very proud. What I wondered was not why you wear them, but if you remove them when you sleep at night?"

Christie nodded. "Yesss."

"How well do you hear without them?"

"Not very well; mostly loud noises only."

Reggie, who'd been making notes on his pad, made one more entry and closed it. "Thank you very much for your time. I'll let you get back to your work now."

"No problem. Goodbye."

When Christie was gone, Rick appeared unsettled. "If you don't mind me asking, why the questions about her hearing?"

"Simple. I was trying to determine if it was possible for someone to be gone without her knowing they left."

*Office of
Lieutenant Jerry Davis
Area 5 Precinct
3:15 p.m.*

Lieutenant Davis sat staring at the papers in front of him, trying to digest what Reggie had just told him. "It looks like you're onto something here, but you need more. He can claim he just happened to be in the same areas, they're popular places, and it's a freak coincidence."

"I doubt a jury would believe that."

Jerry studied his friend. "I doubt the prosecutor would even take this to a jury."

"Let's get his DNA and compare it to the first victim."

"With a warrant?"

Reggie nodded.

"I'm not certain I could even get one, and if you're wrong, we may be alienating our best connection to the killer."

Reggie sighed. "Perhaps I could get his DNA without his knowledge."

"How?"

"I don't know. Maybe if I meet him at a restaurant, I could collect a cup or utensil, something like that."

The lieutenant shrugged. "It's worth a shot. You need to pin down his story and lock him in on where he was when he got those calls."

"I'll call him and arrange a meeting."

"Good. Keep me informed so I can do the same with the chief."

Yard House
North Clybourn Avenue
4:45 p.m.

On the border between the Old Town and Goose Island neighborhoods was the Yard House pub and restaurant. Reggie had easily found a table at the industrial-style sports bar, and after a fifteen-minute wait, Chad showed up. The reporter had a backpack over his shoulder and Reggie immediately sensed a difference in the reporter's demeanor.

"Thanks for meeting me, Chad."

"Sure, sure. Christie told me you went to see her today."

"Yes. She's a very nice girl."

"Yeah, I was lucky to find her when I came to Chicago. Did you get the information you needed?"

"She was very helpful."

A waitress came up to the table and interrupted. "Can I get you something?"

Reggie was already nursing a beer. "You want a cold beer, Chad?"

"No, thanks." He looked up at the waitress. "Do you have bottled water?"

"Sure."

"I'll take that."

"Okay."

Once she was gone, Reggie tried to hide his frustration. He'd planned to save Chad's glass, but the bottle would work if Chad didn't take it with him.

"I wanted to meet in order to make sure there's been no new contact from our guy?"

Chad shook his head. "Not a peep. I assure you you'll get the information first."

"Good."

"Are you making any progress on finding the guy?"

Reggie nodded. "Some."

The bottled water arrived with a glass. Chad accepted the bottle. "I won't need the glass, thanks."

When both the girl and the glass were gone, Chad sipped his water, then turned

242

back to Reggie. "What about the sketch? Anything come of it?"

"Off the record?"

"Of course."

"Not really. We got a bunch of vague tips, and there's a detective following up on them, but I'm not too hopeful."

Chad absently peeled at the label on the bottle. "Vince told me you took a DNA swab from him."

Reggie sensed he better tread carefully. "Yeah. Don't tell him, but that was more to rattle his cage than anything. I didn't like the pressure he put on you to delay the transfer of information."

Chad laughed. "It sure pissed him off!"

The waitress showed up again. "Another beer?"

Reggie slid his glass toward her. "Yeah, thanks. New water, Chad?"

"No, I'm good, thanks."

The girl disappeared and returned moments later with a fresh glass. Meanwhile, most of the label was gone from Chad's bottle, but only half the water. They made small talk for about fifteen minutes, until Reggie decided he wasn't getting anywhere. He polished off his beer and stood. "Well Chad, I better get home to Sonya. Your water is on my tab."

243

"Thanks. Where's the bathroom?"

Reggie pointed near the back, where one of the exits was. "Over there."

"Okay. Thanks again."

Reggie laid some money on the table as he watched Chad walk to the bathroom, the bottle still in his hand. As soon as he was out of sight, Reggie bolted for the exit and circled around by the exit next to the bathroom. Staying out of sight, he waited for Chad to come out.

Just a few minutes later, Chad exited the restaurant, still holding the bottle. Stopping at a nearby trash can, he tossed it in. Reggie held his breath as he watched Chad head to his car, then drive away.

His heart pounding, Reggie went directly to the can. Lying on top was a water bottle with the label peeled off. Taking an evidence bag and turning it inside out, he picked up the bottle, and wrapped it up.

Sealing the top of the bag, he headed for his car, and the forensic lab.

<u>Tuesday, September 16</u>

Homicide Squad Room
Area 5 Precinct
9:15 a.m.

Reggie had been at his desk for nearly two hours, just waiting. He'd dropped off the water bottle at the lab, and because of the immediate threat to lives, they started processing it at once. Still, it took time and Reggie was impatient.

Several cups of coffee, which only frazzled his nerves further, washed down multiple donuts. He tried staring at the phone and forcing it to ring, but that didn't help either. Finally, the coffee took its toll, and he had to go to the bathroom.

When he returned, Jerry called to him from his office. "I got your result!"

It took two steps before Reggie was standing over his boss. "Well, out with it!"

"No match."

Reggie wasn't convinced he heard correctly. "Did you just say no match?"

"That's right; the DNA on the bottle did not match the sample from victim one."

Reggie slumped into the nearest chair. "Are they sure?"

Jerry grinned, despite the bad news. "Thorsen said to tell you she's sure."

Reggie snorted. "Well, Marshall has to be tied to this thing somehow."

"I agree, but the sample may not have been the key to getting an arrest, anyway."

"I'm sorry?"

Jerry leaned forward and crossed his arms on the desk. "After our conversation yesterday, I put in a call to the county prosecutor. I told her what we had and that we were trying to secure a DNA match to victim one's sample."

"Okay, and?"

"She asked where the victim sample came from and I told her the fingernails. Then she wanted to know if Marshall could have had any other contact with her, other than the murder?"

Reggie's mind jumped ahead and suddenly he knew where the prosecutor was going. "You told her Chad found the body, and therefore, he can claim he was checking the victim's condition and was accidentally scratched."

Davis nodded. "Preposterous, I know, but she claimed she wouldn't take it to a jury with just that and the phone calls."

Reggie groaned. "Unbelievable!"

The two were still commiserating about the state of the case when the lieutenant's phone rang. "Homicide; Lieutenant Davis."

Jerry listened for a moment, then glanced up at Reggie. "Yeah, he's here. Okay, send him up."

Jerry hung up. "Chad Marshall is here to see you."

Reggie lifted an eyebrow. "Speak of the devil."

"Indeed."

A few moments later, Chad was standing in the office door. Reggie waved him in. "What's up, Chad?"

"I got another message."

Reggie sat up straight. "Another body?"

"No. Another warning."

Jerry stood and closed his office door. "Play it."

Chad pulled out his phone and put it on speaker.

"I've selected my next victim. She will die like the others. You can tell the press and

warn the people, but it won't stop the inevitable."

The room was silent for a moment. Chad handed a flash drive and a piece of paper to Reggie. "I've gotta run. Vince is waiting on me to do a report for the news at noon."

"Thanks for bringing it by, Chad."

The reporter nodded and left.

Jerry groaned. "What now, Reggie? Have you got a plan B?"

"I've got one person connected to the case I haven't interviewed yet."

"Who's that?"

"Tommy Castillo."

"What's his connection?"

"He's Chad's cameraman."

WWND-10 Studios
North Center
11:00 a.m.

Reggie approached the reception desk and waited for the young man to get off the phone. When the call ended, his attention focused on the detective. "Welcome to WWND. How can we help you?"

Reggie didn't show his badge. There was no sense in setting off alarm bells. "I'm looking for Tommy Castillo."

The receptionist, his nametag identifying him as Phillip, picked up the phone. "Can I tell him your name?"

"Reggie Brown."

Phillip punched a few numbers. "Is Tommy back there?"

A few moments of waiting. "Will you tell him Reggie Brown is at the front desk wanting to speak to him?"

Another pause. "Okay, thanks."

Phillip hung up. "He's on his way."

Reggie moved over by the large front windows and admired the colors surrounding the large WWND campus. So far, it had been a beautiful fall, his favorite season of the year.

"Detective?"

Reggie turned around to see Tommy coming toward him. "Hi, Tommy. Thanks for seeing me."

"Of course. What's this about?"

"Is there somewhere we can talk privately?"

"I was cleaning my equipment in a spare conference room; will that work?"

"That will be fine."

Reggie followed the cameraman down a dimly lit hallway and into a small meeting room. Spread out on the table was a disassembled camera, surrounded by cleaning cloths and sprays. Tommy sat and Reggie grabbed the chair across from him. Reggie's gaze was instantly drawn to a water bottle sitting in front of Tommy, the label mostly peeled away. "You do that all the time?"

"What?"

"Peel the labels off your water bottles?"

Tommy looked down at the bottle and grinned. "Yeah, kind of a habit. It started in college with beer bottles, but I stick with water these days." He laughed. "It drives Chad nuts when I leave little scraps of paper on his desk."

Like a light bulb coming on, Reggie realized whose DNA was on the water bottle from the restaurant. Chad had guessed that if Reggie wanted Vince's DNA, he might want his, and brought another bottle with him to swap.

Reggie played a bluff. "So Tommy, your DNA has surfaced in the investigation of the college girl's murders."

The detective let the statement hang out there on its own as neither a question nor an accusation. The impact on the young man was immediate.

"*My* DNA? What… How?"

"I'm not at liberty to say, but it brings up the question, are you involved with these murders?"

Tommy's eyes grew to size of half-dollars and panic took hold. "No… No way, man. I could never do something like that! You've got it all wrong."

"Really? Set me straight then."

"I told you guys to look at Chad. He's the one you need to investigate."

Reggie held up one of his big hands. "Hold on a sec. When did you tell us to look at Chad?"

"A few days ago. I left a message on that tip line."

"You were the one who told us to look at his previous reports?"

"Yeah… yeah, that was me. I had seen his previous work and it just seemed too weird."

Tommy's reaction struck the veteran detective as sincere. For the moment, he was going to give him the benefit of the doubt. "Okay Tommy, let's say that the previous reports weren't just a coincidence. Why? What would be Chad's motive?"

"Simple; money."

"How would he profit from killing these girls? Surely the little bit of attention wouldn't be worth the risk?"

Tommy snorted. "Don't kid yourself, Detective. Do you know how much national anchors and feature reporters make a year?"

Reggie shrugged. "Never thought about it."

"Well, you should. Seven figures, easily."

The surprise must have shown on Reggie's face, because Tommy started nodding his head. "That's right. If Chad, or any other reporter, can catch the eye of New York and snag a position there, it can mean millions of dollars."

Reggie scoffed. "Are you sure? That seems awful high."

Tommy reached over and opened a laptop. Pulling up Google, he typed in *national anchor pay*. When the results popped up, he turned it toward Reggie. "See that name there?"

Tommy was pointing at the name of Myles Hardy. Reggie nodded and Tommy clicked on the link.

The news story that popped up was about a new contract signed by the ABC national anchor. The deal was for twenty-five million a year. Tommy was watching the detective's reaction. "Now do you see why it's not so out of the realm of possibility?"

Reggie's mind was spinning. "You've made your point, Tommy. Do you happen to know where Chad is now?"

"He was having an extended lunch with Reilly."

"The news director?"

"Yeah, and Vince."

"Tell me this; would his A.P. go with Chad if the reporter got moved to New York?"

"Not necessarily, but it could happen."

"What about his cameraman?"

Tommy actually managed a laugh. "I wish, but no way."

Reggie put away his notepad and stood, extending his hand to the young man. "Thanks for your help."

"You're welcome."

They shook hands, but before Reggie released him, he had one more thing to ask. "Keep the content of this conversation private, will you please?"

"Of course."

Back out at his car, Reggie called the lieutenant. "Homicide; Lieutenant Davis."

"Jerry, it's me. I need a warrant."

"What for?"

"Chad's DNA."

"I'm not sure I can get it."

Reggie filled his boss in on what he had learned from the cameraman.

"No kidding?"

"No kidding. Marshall is due back anytime, so I'm going to wait for him. Let me know when the warrant is on its way."

"Will do."

****

Forty-five minutes later, Chad Marshall, Vince Henderson, and Shawna Reilly all climbed out of the same car in front of the studio. Reggie watched them walk into the building, and it was obvious they were in high spirits. Reggie fought to control his anger, the vision of each of those girls flashing through his memory over and over again. First, their joyous graduation photos, followed quickly by the crime scene shots.

When his phone rang, he snatched open. "Brown!"

"The warrant is on its way with an officer."

"Good. Our boy just showed up."

****

Another forty-five minutes, and Reggie was standing in front of Phillip at the front desk again. This time, when the young man looked up, Reggie had his badge out. "Detective Brown to see Chad Marshall."

"Uh… Okay."

A phone call and a nod of the head. "He'll be right up."

Reggie stayed by the desk this time, and when Chad came through the door, Reggie moved directly toward him. The smile on Chad's face quickly disappeared when he saw the detective. "What's up, Reggie?"

Reggie handed the piece of paper to him, then reached in his pocket for the swab kit. "That's a warrant for your DNA; open your mouth please."

He didn't have to ask twice because Chad's mouth was already hanging open, the combination of shock and fear playing across his face. In that moment, Reggie knew he had his man.

Five minutes later, Reggie had his sample and was back out at his car. With his adrenaline surging, he spun the car out of the parking lot, and headed for Janet Thorsen's lab.

CHICAGO HOMICIDE

<u>Wednesday, September 17</u>

Homicide Squad Room
Area 5 Precinct
9:45 a.m.

Jerry Davis sat behind his desk watching his friend. For the last two hours, Reggie had drank coffee, paced, drank more coffee, sat down at his own desk, drank more coffee, then started pacing again. At that moment, Reggie was sitting in front of him, moaning about how long it was taking. "Man, I can't believe we still haven't heard."

Jerry was anxious too, but much less so than his friend. "Come on, Reg. We can both remember when DNA took months to process. If you had to wait that long, what would you be doing now?"

Reggie thought about it. "Probably going to make-up shops. I still have a few left to check on."

"Then why don't you do that. It'll help both of us."

Reggie fixed his boss with a sideways glare. "What are you saying? Am I bothering you?"

Jerry laughed. "No, you're not bothering me. However, I'm not getting any work done while I'm watching you go nuts, either."

Reggie relaxed and let a smile work its way across his face. "You're probably right. I'm making myself crazy, too."

The lieutenant's phone rang and Reggie went to grab it only to find his hand landing on top of Jerry's. "It's my phone, Reg. I can get it."

Reggie smiled, retracting his hand. "Of course."

Jerry answered it while grinning at Reggie. "Homicide; Lieutenant Davis."

A brief pause, then a nod. "Hi, Janet."

Jerry and Reggie locked eyes. "Hold on, Doc. I'm putting you on speaker." He hit the speaker button and hung up the receiver. "Okay, Janet. Reggie's listening with me, so let us have it!"

"It matched."

Reggie pumped his fist in the air. "Yes!"

Jerry spoke over him. "Solid match?"

"Very. Chad's DNA was under the fingernails of Mackenzie Addison."

"Thanks for the rush job, Doc."

"Always glad to help."

Jerry disconnected the call. "So, what does that give us?"

Reggie was vibrating with released tension. "Motive, opportunity because of a weak alibi, and a physical connection to victim one."

"Okay. Get your files while I contact the prosecutor's office."

When Reggie returned, County Prosecutor Mandy Green was already on the line. "Detective Brown is joining us, Mandy. I'll let him present the case to you."

"Good morning, Detective. I'm ready when you are."

Reggie laid his file on Jerry's desk and opened it. "Good morning, Miss Green."

Thirty minutes later, Reggie finished. He and Jerry waited for the prosecutor to respond, which she did after just a few minutes pause.

"Do we have any physical evidence tying Marshall to the other two victims?"

Reggie shook his head, a strong sense of dread coming over him. "Nothing confirmed."

"What do you mean by confirmed?"

"The coroner discovered a particular kind of make-up on the neck of victim three, but I haven't been able to confirm a source or who purchased it."

Another pause.

"Alright gentlemen, here's the biggest issue. We have nothing physical to tie Marshall to the victims. The DNA match from victim one has been compromised by the fact he discovered the body. The phone records and weak alibi are compelling but still circumstantial."

Reggie's anxiety level was escalating quickly. "What about the pattern of behavior indicated by the news reports?"

"You mean the kidnapped eight-year-old?"

"Yeah."

"Marshall wasn't a suspect in that case. More than likely, a judge wouldn't even allow a jury to hear it."

Reggie slumped in his chair as Jerry took over the call. "Tell us what you need, Mandy."

"One of two things, preferably both. I need physical evidence to tie Marshall to the women, or a witness who saw him with them."

"Okay. Anything else?"

She laughed. "A confession would be nice!"

Jerry nodded. "We'll do what we can. Thanks for your help."

"Anytime."

The line went dead and Jerry leaned back in his chair, studying Reggie. "You know I can pass the case on, Reggie. You don't have to torture yourself any longer."

Reggie stood. "I still have work to do, and I still have some time. I'll let you know when you can pass it on."

Jerry nodded. "That's what I thought you'd say."

Chicago Costume
Portage Park
West Montrose Avenue
11:45 a.m.

Three stores remained on Reggie's list that carried theatrical quality make-up. Two were *Chicago Costume* stores and the other was named *Fantasy Costumes.* The Chicago Costume location in Portage Park was only ten minutes from the Fantasy Costume store, making the decision of where to start simple.

Reggie walked into Chicago Costume to find row upon row of masks, wigs, and every sort of prop he could imagine for getting dressed up. A young lady paused from hanging yet another row of masks. "Can I help you?"

Reggie produced his badge. "I would like to speak with the manager."

"Through that door, up the stairs, and to the right."

"Thank you."

At the top of the stairs, Reggie found a man in his mid-fifties, his ring of gray hair sticking out in all directions as he pounded numbers into a calculator. "Excuse me."

The man looked up, surprised to have a visitor. "Oh, hey. Can I help you?"

"A girl said I could find the manager up here."

"That's me; Sergio Benitez."

Reggie produced his badge again. "Detective Brown; Chicago PD."

Sergio remained fixed in position, his fingers still poised over the calculator. "What can I do for you, Detective?"

"I'm investigating a string of murders, and I was hoping to get some information from your records."

The mention of the word murder changed the man's demeanor immediately. He sat back in his chair and directed his full attention to his visitor. "Wow, okay. What do you need?"

"Do you sell theater-quality make-up?"

"Yes. What in particular?"

Reggie took out his notepad and read off the description. "I'm looking to find out if anyone recently purchased a wax-based, water-activated black."

"Well, the only one I carry matching those specifics is a Wolfe Hydrocolor, but I hardly ever sell it."

"Why is that?"

"Because most people will buy a make-up palette consisting of a black and two or three other colors, and those tend to be cream compounds."

"Can you check on the sales of the Wolfe Hydrocolor?"

"Sure." He pulled a computer keyboard closer to him and punched in some information. After a few seconds, he looked back at the detective. "I have two in stock and haven't sold it since this past January."

Reggie put away his notepad, frustrated. "Okay. Thanks for your help."

"Of course."

Fantasy Costumes
North Milwaukee Avenue
12:10 p.m.

Reggie ignored the grumbling of his stomach and pushed on to his next stop. Fantasy Costumes took up an entire strip mall on a triangular corner. Inside, a similar line-up of products as his previous stop were available, only in much larger quantities. From the front door, aisles stretched out of sight in several directions.

He turned to the young man working the checkout counter. "Is the manager in?"

"Which department?"

"Uh… make-up?"

"Go down this aisle all the way to the end; you'll see a sign hanging from the ceiling."

"Thank you."

"Certainly."

Reggie followed the employee's directions until he arrived at the overhead sign. Standing behind an L-shaped glass counter, a woman in her mid-forties with short black hair and green eyes was helping a customer look through a catalogue.

Reggie bided his time, ignoring the ongoing complaints of his stomach, until the manager was finished. She looked up at Reggie. "May I help you?"

"I'm looking for the manager of the make-up department."

"That's me; I'm Glenna Baxter."

Reggie showed his badge. "I'm Detective Brown with Chicago PD." He put away his badge and pulled out his notebook. "I need information on a particular type of theater make-up."

"Okay." Glenna smiled at the detective. "Can you be more specific?"

Reggie returned the smile and described the product in question.

"Yes, I'm familiar with it. Wolfe Hydrocolor is the only brand we sell that matches that description. Black, you said?"

"Yes, ma'am."

"My sales records are at the other end of the counter. Do you mind following me?"

"Not at all."

They moved to the far end of the thirty-foot counter, and she opened a laptop. After entering a couple numbers, her voice carried an element of surprise. "I don't sell it often, but my last sale was only two weeks ago."

Reggie pulse picked up its pace. "Do you have a record of who purchased it?"

Glenna shook her head. "It was a cash purchase made on August thirty-first."

"Did you help the customer?"

Another shake of short black hair. "No, Karen did."

"Is she here?"

"As matter of fact, yes. Let me get her."

Reggie impatiently stared after the woman as she walked into a back room and disappeared. Less than a minute later, Glenna returned with a blonde girl in her early twenties. "This is Karen Grissom, she took care of the customer."

"Hi, Karen."

"Hey."

"Karen, do you remember selling some black Wolfe Hydrocolor a few weeks ago?"

"Yeah."

"Do you remember who you sold it to?"

"Yeah."

"Could you describe him?"

"Yeah."

Reggie tried to maintain his calm, despite the girl's apparent inability to put two words together. "What did he look like?"

"Well, I didn't recognize him at the time."

Finally, a whole sentence. "Okaaay… but?"

"But I've seen him on TV several times since."

Reggie tried to keep his eyes from bulging out of his head. "On TV?"

"Yeah."

"Karen, would you mind telling me who it was?"

"The TV newsman; the one doing the stories about those poor college girls."

Reggie thought his head would explode. Forcing himself to stay focused, he pushed Karen a little more. "Are you sure?"

"Yeah."

"Did he say what he wanted the make-up for?"

"No."

"Did he say anything?"

"Not really."

Reggie had a photo of Chad with him. "Karen, is this the man?"

"Yeah."

Reggie looked up at Glenna. "Can I get a copy of the receipt?"

"Of course."

While she went after the copy, Reggie smiled down at Karen. "You may have just helped all of those girls get justice. You're absolutely sure of your statement?"

Suddenly, Karen was verbose. "I'm sure, Detective. Absolutely, one hundred percent positive. I'd swear to it on a stack of Bibles and my grandfather's grave."

Reggie stifled a laugh. "I appreciate it, Karen."

Glenna returned and handed the copy to Reggie. He took it and nodded to both women. "Thank you very much, and I'll be in touch soon."

Then he turned and bolted for his car.

WWND-10 Studios
North Center
2:15 p.m.

Chad took a deep breath, then pushed the speaker button on the phone in his office. "This is Chad Marshall."

"Afternoon, Chad. This is Carter Nelson; I'm executive producer of the ABC national news."

"Yes, sir. Nice to meet you."

"Likewise. Chad, we've been watching your reports over the last six or seven months, and frankly, we're impressed. Your work on the kidnapping case was good, but your handling of the Pledge Pin killings has been first rate."

"Thank you for saying so, sir."

"I have a position open for a national correspondent, and I was wondering if you'd be interested in coming to New York."

Chad forced himself to take a breath before answering. "Mr. Nelson, I am flattered and I would be very interested in coming to New York."

"Excellent, and call me Carter."

"Very well, Carter…"

At that moment, the door to Chad's office exploded inward. A uniformed officer and Detective Brown surged into the room, followed by a panicked receptionist. "I'm sorry, Mr. Marshall. I tried to tell him you were on an important call."

The detective dropped a sheet of paper on Chad's desk. "Chad Marshall, this is a warrant to search your vehicle. You can accompany us now or we will perform the search without you present."

Chad stared at the detective in shock, seemingly frozen in mid-sentence.

A voice came over the speaker. "Marshall, what in heaven's name is going on there?"

"Uh… nothing, Mr. Nelson. I need to take care of something. Can I call you back?"

"No, you can't call me back. Explain yourself!"

"I'm sorry, sir. It's something I have to do." Chad reached over and disconnected the call. Reggie was already on his way back out of the office, leaving Chad scrambling to catch up.

****

The big detective was moving with purpose, each step vibrating his entire body as he moved out into the parking lot. He could hear Chad behind him. "Detective! Reggie! What is this all about?"

Reggie ignored him, and was pleased to find Chad's car unlocked when he tried the driver's door. Chad came running up to him. "Now, hold on a second, Reggie. Can't we discuss this?"

Reggie turned to the uniformed officer. "Restrain Mr. Marshall if he gets any closer."

"Yes, sir."

Tommy Castillo and his camera had appeared from nowhere and had begun filming the scene. Reggie looked at Chad, then pointed to the camera. "Look, Marshall! The storyteller has become the story."

Reggie put on latex gloves and started his search in the front seat. He looked under the dash, the seats, the floor mats, and then in the creases between the seats. Moving to the back, he repeated the steps in the rear compartment.

Next, going around to the other side, he popped open the glove box. A small container fell out onto the floor. Reggie picked it up and read the back. *Wolfe Hydrocolor—black.*

He turned toward Chad, who had suddenly lost his voice. "Have you been working in the theater lately, Marshall?"

Reggie dropped the container into an evidence bag, then went back around to the driver's side to push the trunk release. With the trunk lid popped, Reggie began methodically combing through the trunk area, checking for any sign of blood or other material. When he found nothing readily visible to the naked eye, he lifted the carpet that covered the spare tire, then stopped.

For a long moment, he stared at it. The golden ticket as far as evidence went, but at the same time, it represented torture and death. Slowly, he reached in and extracted the double-loop garrote from its hiding place. Dropping it into an evidence bag, he held it up for Chad to see.

271

"Officer, please handcuff Mr. Marshall. He's under arrest for three counts of murder. Then read him his rights and get him out of my sight."

<u>Thursday, September 18</u>
<u>Retirement Day</u>

Home of
Sonya & Reggie Brown
Eastside Neighborhood
7:00 a.m.

"Reggie, are you ready yet?"

"Yes, dear."

"Don't you 'yes-dear' me!"

He leaned over and kissed her cheek. "From today on, whatever you want is yes."

"Oh, well in that case, 'yes, dear' will be just fine."

He laughed and followed her out to the car. "You don't have to do this, you know?"

"I want to. We've worked toward this day together, and I want to share it with you."

"I'm glad."

Reggie climbed into the passenger seat of Sonya's car and allowed himself to be chauffeured to work. He'd always thought he would dread the day he had to hang up his badge, but it didn't feel that way. He was ready.

When they arrived at the precinct, Reggie kissed his wife's cheek and got out. "I'll call you when I'm done."

"Okay. I'm just gonna run some errands."

He closed the car door and started up the walk to the station. When he got to his desk, there was a box of donuts, a vase of flowers, and several phone messages from well-wishers. Despite doing all he could to keep things low-key, there were no secrets in the department.

He responded to some emails, spoke with multiple people who stopped by his desk, and then gathered all his personal items into a cardboard box. It seemed impossible to put thirty years of police work into a single box, but there it was.

His next stop was the personnel office. As with all retiring officers, he was asked to give an exit interview, suggesting what was good, bad, or needs improvement in the department. His statements were generic and positive; the last thing he wanted was to dump on people as his final act at the department.

When he returned to get his belongings, Jerry had arrived. Reggie leaned in the door. "I guess this it, old friend."

Jerry waved him inside. "Come in here and sit down for a minute."

Reggie grabbed what was left of the donuts, setting the open box on Jerry's desk. "Donut?"

"Always."

Reggie grabbed one as well. "What's the status of the Marshall case?"

Jerry paused to answer before devouring his donut. "I talked to Prosecutor Green this morning. She feels there's no charges to be brought against Vince Henderson, both because of his strong alibi at the time of the Addison murder, and because he had no connection with Marshall during the kidnapping stories in Sioux Falls."

Reggie nodded. "Makes sense. I called the Sherriff in South Sioux Falls. He's going to look at Marshall for the kidnapping case up there."

"Good. Marshall deserves all the trouble he gets. I've turned your case over to Franklin for the final interviews and such."

"I saw. I put together an email and sent it to him first thing."

"I guess you turned in your weapon at the exit interview?"

"Yeah. I never liked it much anyway. I prefer my old .357 Magnum."

Jerry laughed. "Hard to change some of us old-timers."

"I guess I'll need to testify at the trial?"

"Yeah, if you can fit it into your busy retirement schedule."

Reggie smiled. "You'll have to clear it with the boss."

They sat quietly for a few minutes, comfortable together after so many years, and not wanting to rush the moment.

Jerry appeared to remember something. "You have your surgery tomorrow, right?"

"Yeah; heck of a way to start my retirement."

"Make sure you call and let us know how it went."

"I will, or at least, Sonya will. I'm sure everything will be fine."

"The department has a big bash planned for you at the Ridgemoor Country Club on the twenty-eighth. It should be fun."

"I'd rather they didn't. You know I don't like all that attention."

"Yeah, but the brass need an excuse to eat and drink!"

Someone appeared at the door. "There you are!"

The men turned to see Janet Thorsen holding a box of donuts. "I wanted to come

276

by and see you off. I'll be on vacation when they're roasting you at Ridgemoor."

Reggie accepted the donuts and laid them on the desk next to the first box. "Thanks, Doc."

"Don't mention it."

Reggie looked at Jerry. "Did I tell you I'm the one who finally got her to smile at a crime scene?"

"No, you didn't mention it. Surely you're mistaken!"

Jerry was grinning at him, and when Reggie looked at the coroner, she was grinning as well. "Okay, what's going on here?"

Jerry laughed. "Thorsen has been smiling at crime scenes ever since she started here, except yours, that is."

Reggie looked from his friend to Janet, and back again. "What are you talking about?"

Jerry pointed at Janet. "Ask her."

Reggie turned to the coroner. "What are you grinning at, Thorsen?"

She laughed. "The first time we met at a crime scene, I was really nervous, but you kept cracking jokes trying to get me to smile. It seemed to torture you that I didn't laugh, so I kept a straight face the next time; seven-plus years later and I was still at it, until the other day."

Reggie looked at Jerry for confirmation. He could see it in his friend's eyes. "You knew about this?"

"Pretty much everybody did."

Reggie shook his head and broke into laughter, pointing at the coroner. "I never would have guessed. I thought you were the most serious person at a scene I'd ever met."

Her faced turned grave. "Oh, I am, Reggie. I am!"

They all cracked up together, and Reggie stood. "On that note, I'm outta here!"

****

When Sonya drove up in the parking lot, Reggie was waiting with his box. Putting it in the back seat, he climbed in. "Stay busy?"

She smiled at him. "Look in the glovebox."

He popped it open to find a manila envelope with both their names on it. "What's this?"

"Open it."

Eyeing her suspiciously, he undid the clasp and slid out the contents. Two plane tickets to Puerto Rico and a hotel brochure for the Copamarina Beach Resort landed in his lap. "What's all this?"

"That is your surgery recovery plan."

"You bought tickets and a hotel room in San Juan?"

She kissed his cheek. "Nope, you did. I told you if your retirement went past the due date, it would cost you dearly!"

He stared at her, then laughed. "Yes, yes you did!"

Author's Note

As always, let me first thank each and every one of you who have made time to read CHICAGO HOMICIDE. I hope you have found it worth your effort.

Many of you have written to say you enjoy the series and there is no greater incentive to keep writing than those letters. You'll never know how much they're appreciated.

More HOMICIDE books are planned, including Dallas, Denver, Seattle, and others. (Not necessarily in that order!) I attempt to give the reader a look at the city as well as solving the crime, and the research has proved to be very interesting. I hope you have enjoyed that part of the books as well. If Chicago is your home, or any of the other cities, I hope the descriptions have been true to the realities.

Until the next book, happy reading and thanks again.

God Bless, John
I John 1:9

Cover by Beverly Dalglish
Edited by Samantha Gordon, Invisible Ink Editing
Proofreading by Robert Toohey

John C. Dalglish

Other Clean Suspense Books

By

John C. Dalglish

THE CITY MURDERS SERIES

BOSTON HOMICIDE - #1
MIAMI HOMICIDE - #2
CHICAGO HOMICIDE - #3

THE DETECTIVE JASON STRONG SERIES

"WHERE'S MY SON?" - #1
BLOODSTAIN - #2
FOR MY BROTHER - #3
TIED TO MURDER - #5
ONE OF THEIR OWN - #6
DEATH STILL - #7

CHICAGO HOMICIDE

THE CHASER CHRONICLES

TORN BY THE SUN - (HISTORICAL FICTION)

Made in the USA
Middletown, DE
01 September 2018